SUNSET IN SIERRA LEONE

SUNSET IN
SIERRA LEONE

Michael Nicolas Wundah

The Book Guild Ltd
Sussex, England

First published in Great Britain in 2004 by
The Book Guild Ltd
25 High Street
Lewes, East Sussex
BN7 2LU

Copyright © Michael Nicolas Wundah 2004

Typesetting in Baskerville by
SetSystems Ltd, Saffron Walden, Essex

Printed in Great Britain by CPI Bath

A catalogue record for this book is
available from The British Library

ISBN 1 85776 843 4

*This book is dedicated to the memories of
the following people:
My dead parents – Tamba Ebrima
Wundah and Sia Tuwor Wundah.
My daughter Michaella Hawa Wundah,
who died in tragic circumstances in
Freetown, Sierra Leone. All those who died
during the brutal civil war in Sierra Leone.
To the British Government, Aid
Organisations and the International
community for supporting the return of
peace to wartorn Sierra Leone.
Finally, to exponents of the advancement of
a quality, functional education, human
rights, positive patriotism, national
reconciliation and good governance in
post-war Sierra Leone.*

M.N.W.

Acknowledgements

I owe the writing of this book to many people, including my families; distinguished personalities, friends and students at Lambeth College. They all helped me in various ways.

First, my two little boys – Ebrima Tamba Wundah and Wahkar Nyuma Wundah. Ebrima helped me with words search in the dictionary. As for Wahkar, his mum and I often say that he brought me luck and strength, for after his birth, I gathered more strength and inspiration and worked smoothly with renewed confidence and determination. Their cousin Haddy Saine was also helpful. Bravo to the three of them!

Second, My principal Ian Ashman, the Assistant principal, School of Community Education, Danny Ridgeway, and the Head of Community Education, Dawn Benson for their support. They deserve my sincere thanks.

Third, my students at the Brixton Centre and School of Community Education, Adare Centre, Lambeth College of Further Education, London. As Adult learners I gained a lot from their experiences.

Finally, I must thank my wife Aji Sarr-Wundah, who doesn't see much more of me than a hunched back, over a computer. But as always, she has helped me with research, given me the benefit of her sure editorial eye and dispatched my on and off doubts to the abyss. I cannot conceive of writing a book without her, she is my muse.

M.N.W.

1

The New-Age Reformer

When the telephone first rang, Richard Kpanabom was full of excitement. He jumped to his feet and looked around the room, soon spotting the phone where it sat on top of an old cupboard in the far corner. He hurried towards it, stepping around boxes and furniture, but as he got near it he hesitated to lift the receiver for fear that it might deliver bad news.

He stood still, indecision raging within him. The phone rang and rang. Still he hesitated. Eventually, he made the sign of the Cross, recited two Hail Marys for inspiration and strength, bent over and carefully picked up the receiver.

'Hello?'

'Hello? Gbanabom?'

At first the caller's voice didn't sound familiar. 'Who is this, please?' Kpanabom asked anxiously.

In a rather authoritative voice the caller said: 'Gbanabom, I'm afraid that your application has been turned down. Good day to you.'

It was a short message but immediately had a dramatic effect on Kpanabom. He put the receiver down, took in a deep breath and reflected for almost twenty minutes. Finally, he figured out who the caller was.

'It could be Mr Kamara, the new Secretary General at the Central Office,' he thought to himself.

When the caller had spoken to him, one thing had made an instant and strong impression: the manner in which he had pronounced Kpanabom's name was associated with certain ethno-linguistic peculiarities. Instead of saying 'Kpanabom', he said 'Gbanabom'. Kpanabom knew that in the world of oral communication, there are certain linguistic peculiarities associated with distinct ethnic groups, known as 'ethno-linguistic syndrome'. These peculiarities cut across race, nationality and geopolitical boundaries. For instance, in Sierra Leone, the defect manifests itself in almost all the ethnic groups. Some struggle with 'kpa', 'j' and 'nja'. So 'Kpana' is mispronounced as 'Gbana', 'Joseph' becomes 'Yoosef', 'Njala' is 'Injala' and 'jetty' is 'yetty'. Others have problems with suffixes such as '-tion'. Thus, 'education' is pronounced 'educason' and 'qualification' is pronounced 'qualificason'.

Such a defect had been apparent when Alphonsus Kamara mispronounced Kpanabom's name at his interview. He repeatedly did this, until another of the interview panel, a man called Musa, had to correct him.

'Mr Secretary General, sir, the applicant is not "Gbanabom"; he is called "Kpanabom".' Musa reminded the Secretary General of this fact again a little while later, but he took no real notice. For Kamara knew very well that the entire panel suffered from the same or similar problems.

So, finally, Kpanabom decided that the caller had been Mr Alphonsus Kamara, the new Secretary General of the All People's Congress Party (APC). Kamara was a recent arrival, having been flown home from Moscow, where he had

2

served five years as Education Attaché. He was a robustly-built man, with a small, round head and a carelessly 'styled' moustache. He was cool, calculating and softly-spoken, with a keen intelligence, having a good degree from the Fourah Bay College, University of Sierra Leone.

After university, Kamara worked as a teacher at the Bo Government Secondary School. He successfully taught and shepherded through their exams two years' worth of students, and his success rate was such that he quickly became the darling boy of the School Board and all the parents. As a result, one of the Board members, who served as a senior diplomat in Romania, helped to pave the way for Alphonsus to work in the Diplomatic Service.

His first posting was at the Sierra Leone embassy in Moscow. Kamara proved to be a natural diplomat, and he wrote many important speeches to be read at party conventions. His excellent penmanship and way with words made him as popular in Moscow diplomatic circles as he had been with the pupils, parents and School Board back in Sierra Leone.

But then, suddenly, he was recalled to Sierra Leone. It had been noted that he held radical views about the conduct of his government where higher education and corruption were concerned, and such views could not be tolerated from a diplomat in a foreign land. His claims were far from false. During his time in Moscow he became aware that many scholarships were awarded to undeserving applicants, and that diplomatic passports were being sold to smugglers and the like. As a result, the traditional wing of the APC condemned him and accused him of making it all up to further his career. But their anger, and his recall to his homeland, did not bother Alphonsus Kamara. Neither did these things curtail his career. On the contrary, he soon assumed the role of Secretary General of the party, which remit included the selection of applicants for the Russian academic awards, and Alphonsus vowed to make the selection process 'whiter than white'. He was determined that due and proper process would be observed, no matter what, even if it cost him his job.

At the height of the Cold War, the Soviet Union was a good friend of most Third World countries, particularly those in Africa. However, this 'friendship' had an ulterior motive: the communist grand plan to win over any non-communist nation to their cause.

The USSR was determined to achieve this objective at all costs, because most Third World countries were members of the Non-Alignment Movement. In the face of an extremely confusing bipolar Cold War political rift, this movement wanted to maintain neutrality, at least in principle. However, some countries played the neutrality card very cleverly, and used it as a political ploy to woo the two superpowers at that time: the USSR and the USA, and secure massive foreign aid.

Via a combination of quasi-communism/left-wing socialism and elements of western-style democracy, the APC managed to keep both sides sweet, by trading them off against one another. The result was not just financial aid, but also substantial amounts of arms.

As a staunch supporter of the party, Thomas Josiah Kpanabom, our Kpanabom's uncle, benefited greatly from party perks, which others might call corrupt practices. For example, his nephew believed that he had a right to a Russian scholarship, despite the fact that he was a secondary school dropout. However, neither he, nor his uncle, had counted on resistance and scrutiny from Alphonsus Kamara. Alphonsus, for his part, had decided to be tough on the nephew, and make an example of him.

Hence the brief and terse telephone message.

Young Kpanabom now decided to ring the Secretary General back, for further clarification. His call was transferred to Kamara without delay.

'How may I help you Mr Gbanabom?' he enquired.

'It is in relation to the scholarship interview. I'll be grateful for further clarification, sir'.

'What further clarification do you need? I have already told you that you are not qualified, haven't I made the point?'

There was nothing more to be said. Kpanabom hung up.

Alphonsus replaced the receiver at his end and sighed. He was not surprised that the young man was finding the decision hard to accept. But it was high time that people realised that the bad old days of quick fixes and nepotism were over – at least for as long as he remained Secretary General.

Devastated by the news, which had now finally sunk in, Kpanabom retired immediately to his narrow room, locked the door and threw himself on the hard bed. But he could not rest. He did not know what to do with himself. So he paced the room, and lay down, and paced again, and did not emerge for three long days and nights.

When he could not sleep, he prayed. He was a staunch Roman Catholic, as his parents had been. So he prayed, but it gave him little comfort. He knew he should eat, go out, pull himself together, but he had no appetite for food at that moment; no appetite for life.

His eyes rested on the family photos he had about his room. He burst into tears, saying aloud, 'You are dead and gone forever, and never again shall you go through the cruelties of this unfair life. If there is life after death, as the Bible says, then may thy spirits stand shoulder to shoulder with me; turn this tide of misery and restore victory in my favour, I pray thee, my dead parents.'

He knelt down and made the sign of the Cross, then rose and paced once again.

'So, I don't have the necessary qualifications!' he muttered, more angry than despairing now. 'Who said that this was about qualifications? Kamara doesn't seem to understand that that's not how things work.' Bitterly, he recalled how previous applicants had easily obtained their awards without presenting a single certificate to the panel. In fact, most of them were secondary school dropouts just like himself.

What about Sundifu, Wurie, Jones, Tamba, Nyuma, Finda, Sorie, Kongomanyi, Finnoh? he thought angrily. Did they get their awards on academic merit? Of course not! They were awarded scholarships purely on the basis of their parents' status in the party. It was so unfair!

Someone knocked on the door.

It was Mikalu Kakpata, his team and classmate. Mikalu's parents were as poor as church mice, and they struggled even to survive. Despite this they had paid Mikalu's tuition fees so far by borrowing money, pawning off their small coffee plantation, which Mr Kakpata senior had inherited from his grandparents. All this meant a meagre existence for the rest of the family. And their situation was far from unique.

As for Mikalu, he received regular food subsidies at the house of the Kpanaboms. There were often leftovers. Although Uncle Josiah was not a rich man, he was quite capable of providing a square meal for his household and of sparing some for the needy.

6

The last time Mikalu had seen his Kpanabom was when they had played their last two football matches against the Bombohun and Segbewema primary schools, before the Christmas holidays. Kpanabom had scored two goals at both games, putting his school at the top of the Inter-Primary Schools Football League in the Kailahun District.

There was a lot to talk about. Mikalu was anxious to share and re-live the good memories of the matches. That was the main reason that brought him to the house. He was aware that his friend had attended a Russian scholarship interview, but he didn't know that Kapanabom had been rejected.

Unfortunately, Kpanabom was feeling so ashamed and frustrated by his rejection that he refused to open the door. He didn't want his friend to see him in his wretched state, and he was also afraid that if he told Mikalu about his failure, Mikalu would pass on the bad news to Teresa Cole.

Teresa was the daughter of their Deputy Headmaster, Mr Theo Cole. She was a tall, lanky lady with the romantic eyes of an angel. In the name of love, she would do anything for the football idol who was young Kpanabom and competition for his affections was fierce.

Mikalu knocked on the door for almost thirty minutes; eventually he gave up and left in disappointment.

2

Quantum Leap

No sooner had Mikalu left, there was another knock on the door. At first Kpanabom was hesitant, but when he looked through the spyhole, he realised that it was his uncle, Thomas Josiah. Kpanabom never called his uncle 'Thomas' though; very few people did. To most, he was always known as Josiah, and to Kpanabom as Uncle Josiah.

He opened the door, let his uncle in, and knelt down and greeted him on bended knees, in accordance with custom and tradition.

Uncle Josiah was a hard-core disciplinarian. He detested sentimentalists and often condemned them as weak and feeble-minded.

'Life has no easy options. It is not about tears on the cheap. It knows neither cowardice, nor retreats in the face of major obstacles. This is true for the poor as well as the rich, for stable as well as volatile societies. Those who think otherwise delude themselves. History shall never forgive such people,' he often told his juniors in order to under-score his no nonsense philosophy on life.

In 1967, the APC had come to power. Josiah paved his way into mainstream politics and consolidated his links with members of high society and influential power brokers. In the beginning, his family had not had a good reputation, but as time went on, by the force of his will and the connections he made in society, Josiah had managed to reinstate his family name as one worthy of respect.

In 1981, the APC hosted its grand annual convention in the capital of the northern province, Makeni. Makeni was also one of the party's major strongholds, so it was a spectacular occasion. Mind you, party conventions were always full of pomp and pageant, particularly during the period of one party government in Sierra Leone.

The APC was a popular party, and their conventions usually attracted thousands of party supporters (customarily referred to as 'comrades'). It was also customary for delegates to wear red garments with red party badges firmly pinned or stuck to the right side of their chests. During such conventions, party officials were selected for high offices in the land, such as company directorships, membership of the Central Committee and jobs in the Foreign Office.

Above all, decisions reached at conventions became the official blueprints of government policy. This whole system very much mirrored Soviet political culture, and it suited the regime very well.

Among the handful of delegates selected for membership of the prestigious Central Committee of the party at the 1981 convention was Uncle Josiah. This meant that he now wielded a great deal more power than ever he had before. It was a quantum leap. Henceforth, he continued to enjoy the luxuries of high-ranking party membership.

But it is often said that Rome was not built in a day. Certainly this adage applied to Josiah and his family. It had been a long road, and a hard one. Josiah's life had been a turbulent affair, and his 'quantum leap' was very much one of rags to riches, from obscurity to significance.

When the APC had been in opposition, between 1961 and 1967, Josiah was among those party loyalists thrown into the notorious Pademba Road prison innumerable times without seeing the doors of a courtroom, let alone having a fair trial. The history of the Josiah family was also marked by one personal misfortune after another. Josiah's mother had twelve children, six boys and six girls. They had lived in the village of Benduma, of the Jawai Chiefdom in the Kailahun District. Sadly, ten of the children died in their teenage years.

Josiah's only surviving sister was Faimata, Kpanabom's mother, and she died when she was twenty. Yet another sad statistic among many in that troubled Chiefdom, from which governments had persistently extorted money in the form of unfair taxes, leaving the people with nothing. There were no health care facilities and very little in the way of formal policing. The result was high infant mortality and a soaring crime rate.

The Daru Military Barracks, just across the River Moa, could have helped to solve, at least in part, the health care and other related social problems of the Chiefdom, had things been done in the proper way. With its financial resources, manpower and expertise, it was capable of subsidising educational projects and training community health personnel for the district. Unfortunately, the barracks was not run properly, and provided no assistance to the people.

All in all, the people of Jawai, as was the case for many such areas in the country, had felt no benefits whatsoever from Sierra Leone's political independence, which was attained on 27 April 1961.

When the Sierra Leone People's Party (SLPP) was in power in the 1960s, Jawai Chieftain and Kailahun District produced a Cabinet Minister and an Acting Prime Minister, but these appointments symbolised nothing other than another form of mainstream cosmetic politics, of no practical benefit to the people of the Chiefdom.

Like the SLPP before it, the APC also trumpeted a lot of promises when they came to power. But they failed to translate them into real development projects in the regions. Neither did they succeed in improving or eradicating the chronic social diseases of poverty and inequality. It was easy to look at the APC and recall the events in George Orwell's *Animal Farm*.

In this novel, political deceit, inequality and the dangers of absolute power are beautifully summarised in a single compelling line: 'All animals are equal, but some animals are more equal than others'. That had always been the nature of power relations between the government and the electorate in the Kailahun District.

When Kpanabom's mother died, Uncle Josiah and his wife, Kaema Kallon, adopted the poor orphan. But at forty, and after five years of unstable marriage, Kaema abandoned Uncle Josiah on the grounds that he was partially impotent. Worst of all, they had no children.

So, after a catalogue of traumas, the only person left in the life of Josiah was his nephew, Kpanabom. He was very fond of him, and Kpanabom respected and loved his uncle very much. 'He is my soul, my blood and flesh. He is my strength,' Josiah often consoled himself, whenever his nephew did silly things like any normal teenager.

Unfortunately, Josiah's family had never been academically gifted. Josiah himself had been a school dropout, failing to make the grade for admission to secondary schooling. His sister, Kpanabom's mother, had been a truant, and had failed her examinations and also dropped out of school. She had become pregnant very soon afterwards, and had had Kpanabom at the age of seventeen.

Like his mother before him, the young Kpanabom was also academically poor, but he had a special gift that made him a household name in the Kailahun District: he was a talented footballer. At sixteen, he played for the school and Kailahun District teams. His goals won them many trophies.

Always proud of the footballing talent of his pupil, the Headteacher, Mr Michael Moinina Vandi, gave Kpanabom a nickname: 'Brainy Feet'. And indeed, he did have brainy feet, feet which performed wonders on the football pitch and brought huge happiness to fans and compatriots.

Uncle Josiah had served in the Sierra Leone army, and was stationed at the Moa Barracks, Daru. He was officially known as Private SLA/1815 283211, Thomas Josiah Kpanabom. But despite the fact that he was a dedicated soldier he made no substantial progress. His first hurdle came when he took the non-commissioned officer examination. He failed it miserably, killing off any prospect of promotion. In fact, his service file was relegated to the waste paper baskets of his superiors, and he was written off as a no-hoper.

Thus, throughout his fifteen years of active service, Josiah only managed to reach the rank of Lance Corporal. This frustrated him, and eventually he resigned from the army.

It is often said that there are changes in the affairs of men. So with the passage of time, dramatic changes in Josiah's life produced a momentum characteristic of fairy tales. And the scripts of his life were rewritten.

Two years after his resignation from the army, Josiah picked up a job at the Sierra Leone Produce Marketing Board. He was soon promoted to the rank of Produce Examiner, Grade Two. Henceforth, he was rapidly promoted. And with promotion came lucrative avenues of opportunity to amass wealth and win political power.

After the party convention at Makeni, Josiah couldn't stop thinking about the world of huge opportunities that had opened up in front of him. He was so excited that one evening he took a hard look at his image in the big, old, dressing mirror in the parlour. For a long time he had avoided assessing himself in this mirror, for fear that to do so would bring back painful memories of the bad old days. But now he felt that he could, literally, face himself again.

3

The Hypnosis of Political Power

They say political power often makes certain people arrogant, greedy, stupid, crazy, blind to reality, and brings about their self-destruction. The powers and privileges showered on Josiah at the Makeni convention did indeed go to his head. He looked in his large, old mirror, and considered for a full five minutes the magnitude of his new political status. And he said to himself: 'It is now time to reinvent myself. I must banish all my old misfortunes and bad memories of the army, and get on with my new, much more promising life. With time, and God willing, my nephew and I are bound to make history. It is no longer a dream, but reality. And it has already begun. But I have equally to prepare my nephew in order to make him a fruitful stakeholder in this dream.'

Josiah then called his nephew, only to find that he had locked himself in his room and had not been out for days.

'Why have you become a self-imposed prisoner of late?' he asked. 'You have not even told me the result of your interview since I returned from the convention. Now, tell me, how did it go young man?' He waited patiently for a response, but there was nothing forthcoming. Instead, Kpanabom stood in front of his uncle like a statue, tense and afraid to utter a word.

15

His uncle became concerned. This was not the lively, sharp, focused and always smiling Kpanabom. 'Speak up, nephew, what is wrong with you?' he demanded.

Kpanabom was now in tears, trembling in front of his uncle like a convicted criminal in the presence of a judge. He still stood there, speechless and miserable.

'Well, say something!' His uncle urged forcefully, like a parade commander thundering commands at his squad.

Finally, out came the awful words at last.

'I didn't qualify for the scholarship sir,' Kpanabom said bluntly. He could think of no other way to break the awful news.

Josiah couldn't believe his ears. He did not really believe what he had just heard, and asked Kpanabom again. Kpanabom told him, once again, that he had failed to secure the scholarship.

'You didn't what!' his uncle roared. 'Is this some kind of joke? You can't be serious!'

Josiah looked hard at his nephew, and now saw how terribly run down he was – not only in body, it seemed, but also in spirit. He seemed broken. Josiah reached into his jacket and produced some official-looking documents.

'Look at these nephew.' Kpanabom seemed disinterested. 'Look!' Josiah insisted.

The documents bore the seal of the party and the signatures of the three most prominent party officials. The first signature was that of His Excellency, the President, Chairman and Leader of the party, Dr Siato Probet Siato. He was also Grand Commander of the Order of Rokel, and held the Order of the Mosquito. He was Chancellor of the University of Sierra Leone, Fountain of Honour and Justice and Commander of the armed forces of Sierra Leone.

The second signatory was the Rt Hon. Sikoma, alias

'Satan Incarnate' of the APC. He was the chief strategist, with special responsibilities to 'fix' and rig elections throughout the land. He was also the brains behind the machine of terror that maintained the status quo. He was the First Vice President of Sierra Leone.

The Third signatory was the third in command. He was called Cicato Talla. He was the Second Vice President of the country. Although he didn't have any special responsibilities, like the First Vice President, he was nevertheless a powerful figure in the eyes of the party. Above all, he and the President were of the same tribe. As an ex-serviceman, he was a disciplined politician but tainted by the stigma of his party.

Political commentators often referred to these three political heavyweights as the Father, Son and Holy Ghost of the political empire of Sierra Leone. Like crafty spiders, they wove powerful political webs of infinite length and strength, coaxing willing prey from almost every sector of society. Their power as a triumvirate was absolute, and the people of the country believed them to be invincible. As a result, the regime had managed to squash military coups and civil unrest, and had now been in power for many years.

The documents that Josiah now presented to young Kpanabom were the official colour of the APC: red. They conferred on Josiah many privileges and useful political and legal immunities. Kpanabom read slowly through them and their significance slowly dawned on him. He shook his head in appreciation, overwhelmed by the new opportunities that now opened up for his uncle, and hopefully for himself too.

His uncle smiled, and embraced his nephew, wiping away the remains of his tears. 'Now, I want no more of these,' he said gently. 'I have now secured privileges for us both that will last until we die. We are secure, and you must not fret. Now, I want you to tell me why you think your application has been rejected.'

'Well, sir, while you were away, the Secretary General called here. I know it was him, because I rang back to confirm it, and to confirm what he had said. He told me that I had failed the interview.'

'And did he give you a reason?'

'He said it was because I don't have the necessary qualifications sir.' Kpanabom replied helplessly.

'But that means that your name has been removed from the final list! That list was prepared in my presence before I went to the Makeni convention. You were number ten on the list, after the names of the children of three Cabinet Ministers. The Secretary General must have interpreted the contents of a different list.' Secretly though, Josiah knew he was up against the reforming zeal of Alphonsus Kamara.

'Now you listen to me,' Josiah said to his nephew. 'Your name will be reinstated on the list. I swear it to you. Remember: this is Sierra Leone, and we the APC – we own this country!'

Sadly, he not only believed he was right – he was right. And his new-found power would soon corrupt him as it had corrupted so many before him.

The power of the APC had no limits. If you said the right things, and knew the right people, no matter what your personal abilities might be, you could have whatever you wanted – ministerial appointments, diplomatic assignments, political privileges and immunities. Anything. No one, it seemed, was beyond the web of corruption: not judges, nor lawyers, nor businessmen and women, nor senior members of the armed forces, nor civil servants. Everyone was drawn in, and no one got out – not alive at any rate. All in all it was the most clandestine, well-orchestrated and corrupt political project in the history of Sierra Leone politics. Not even academics were immune. Those who made a stand were ostracised, and the rest adopted the policy of 'When in Rome, do as the Romans do'. It was pathetic, for in the end this philosophy was counterproductive, and most of them were reduced to the degrading status of pseudo-intellectuals.

4

The Conspiracy

Alphonsus Kamara lived in temporary accommodation when he returned to Sierra Leone from the USSR, in a room at the Brookfields Hotel in Freetown. Brookfields was a modest but well-kept social rendezvous, the buildings spread over acres of flat, green land.

At that time, tourism in Sierra Leone was limited, so the facilities at Brookfields attracted mostly the local gentry. They included top politicians, civil servants and the commercial class. Periodically, customers from neighbouring Liberia and far away Europe also passed some time there.

Brookfields was not short of the excitements that usually characterise entertainment centres, local or international. There were regular happy hours, which attracted hundreds of beautiful ladies in glittering high-heeled shoes and colourful miniskirts. Above all, there were well-kept rooms, many rented on a temporary as well as a permanent basis.

However, life at Brookfields could be described as a social theatre with mixed reviews. On the entertainment side, it was second to none, but the entertainments often created the perfect scenarios for heartbreaking disappointments such as broken promises and unfulfilled romance.

The heydays of Brookfields were created by the periods of economic boom in Sierra Leone. During those days, money found its way into almost every pocket, and people spent freely. Corruption was also at its highest. A classic example was the fraudulent syndicates, whereby fake vouchers full of fictitious names, or 'ghost workers', claimed fortunes from the government treasury.

With more than enough 'bad money' in circulation, sensuous enterprises such as promiscuous love nests proliferated *en masse* at various places, including Freetown, Bo, Makeni, Kono, Kenema and in the remote diamond fields of Tongo. People nationwide dubbed this era the 'swinging' days of Sierra Leone.

Alphonsus Kamara, despised and deposed by his political paymasters, tasted part of the 'swinging' days himself, but only for a brief period.

'What is the reason behind this rare, cosy, red-carpet hospitality given to me by the party since I returned from Moscow?' he asked Briget, his sister-in- law. 'I thought the party recalled me as a punishment. Besides, instead of demotion, they have promoted me to the rank of Secretary General.' They were relaxing one evening in one of the main entertainment suites of his hotel. It was, of course, a rhetorical question, for Briget knew nothing of such matters, and besides she had other things on her mind. She wanted to have Alphonsus all to herself and make passionate love to him – something she had longed to do for ages.

She said: 'Why do you bother to ask such silly questions? Stop thinking so negatively about yourself. After all, you were a senior diplomat in Moscow, so you deserve the post of Secretary General, Alphonsus. Always remember that.' Briget didn't know if he deserved it or not, and nor did she care much. But she wanted him at his ease, relaxed, open to seduction.

Their table was littered with whisky glasses and bottles,

22

imported beers and Russian vodka. Since his time in Russia, Alphonsus' taste for spirits other than vodka had diminished considerably. So he helped himself solidly to vodka and lemonade throughout the evening, while Briget gulped the other brands of drink at her disposal.

It was time to enjoy the happy moment, so a lot of seducing took place. Briget sat right in front of Alphonsus, miniskirt facing him and her blouse wide open. Her succulent breasts bulged out. They transfixed the Secretary General, and he found himself powerless to look away.

They drank and danced far into the night. Their anxieties (well, Alphonsus' to be precise) fell away, and they communicated as much through body language as through talk. Soon, Briget thought. Soon he will be ready for me. Shortly after midnight she made her move, unable to contain herself any longer. 'Emotions, romantic feelings, know neither shame, nor borders. There are no ethics in this business,' she whispered to him. 'I'm tired, let's go up.'

His response was not what she had expected. 'Then lets occupy the table by the swimming pool, where you will have the opportunity to relax in an armchair, and enjoy the fresh air,' he suggested.

She reluctantly agreed. Once seated by the pool, she threw caution to the wind and made her move.

Alphonsus acted outraged. 'Stop! Don't you know that you are my sister-in-law?' Secretly, he knew that in the dirty, selfish game of promiscuity, it is always wise to play safe. You could never tell what might happen. He found Briget almost irresistible, and now gazed keenly into her dazzling, romantic eyes. He must not appear *too* keen.

Briget was the younger sister of Alphonsus' wife, Lucia. When she had finished high school, Briget had worked briefly for the Sierra Leone Civil Service as a Temporary

Secretary at the Ministry of Agriculture. Her love life was similar to that of a butterfly: she flirted with virtually all the bosses, especially the Permanent Secretaries. It had earned her the notorious nickname of 'Super Mattress'.

However, because she was from a family that was academically inclined, she was placed under enormous pressure to make sure that no matter what happened in her colourful love life, she must pursue a university education. So when Mr and Mrs Alphonsus Kamara were away in Moscow, Briget eventually undertook further studies at the Fourah Bay College, University of Sierra Leone, and read history and philosophy. She graduated with a third-class honours degree.

As for the relationship between her and Alphonsus, this had quite a history. Before her sister and Alphonsus got married, it was an open secret that she had a crush on him. There were even rumours that Briget would spoil the party for her senior sister, which periodically strained their relationship.

When Alphonsus was recalled from Moscow amid chaos, Briget's passion for him was as fresh as ever. She was very much tempted and anxious to try her luck a second time. Most importantly, she was very confident that the prospects were not only high this time, but much more secure, because Alphonsus had left her sister and the kids behind in Moscow. He instructed them to join him after a couple of months as he needed to make full assessment of the situation.

'Come on baby don't play God! We've kissed before, and I know what you're afraid of. But your goddess is thousands of miles away in Moscow, so we can play the game freely. There is no better chance than this. Now is the time. They say when the cat is away, the mouse plays.'

She tempted him further with a broad smile. Again, her delicate, tempting breasts bulged from the little red blouse as if they were about to land on the lap of the diplomat.

Briget bullishly tried all the tricks in the book of seduction. But initially Alphonsus was diplomatic, conservative, he exercised caution. When they reached a compromise and were about to gravitate into another gear, cushioned particularly by Briget, it was not to be. There was a sudden obstruction, throwing the whole question of the chance to cheat on Mrs Alphonsus Kamara into confusion.

Earlier in the day, Denis Dickson, one-time college mate of Alphonsus, had left a note for him and a spoken message with the chief messenger, Alimamy Gboos Gboos. But apparently, the Saturday happy hour got the better of him, and he forgot to deliver it. It was only when Alphonsus and Briget had changed their sitting position and ordered another round of drinks that Gboos Gboos realised that he had not delivered the note. So he rushed to the reception desk at once and emerged with the note.

'Good evening sir, I have an important message for you, and a note.' Gboos Gboos handed the note and tendered his apologies for the delay.

Alphonsus read it studiously. The contents were worrying. 'And what is the message?'

'Mr Dickson said that no matter how late it is in the night, you must give him a call. He also said that you know his number. He sounded very anxious, sir.'

With an unfavourable letter and an urgent, worrying message, Mr Secretary General was put under enormous pressure immediately. Extremely perplexed, he perspired profusely. His blood pressure increased considerably.

Gboos Gboos then said, 'He said it is very serious and urgent sir. And that the earlier you call, the better.'

Without wasting any time, Alphonsus told the receptionist at the counter to call a cab so that he could dispatch Briget immediately and face his ordeal in the privacy of his hotel room.

Those were the days when time meant money in Sierra Leone. Basic services such as transportation were up and running, at least in certain sectors of society. In less than one minute, the taxi was ready at the main gate of the hotel.

'You must go home immediately,' Alphonsus told his jilted lover. 'I have to attend to urgent business.' He gave her a five-dollar note as her taxi fare, supported by a gentle pat on the back, and bade her goodnight. She was devastated. After all her efforts, it had all ended in another failure.

'Thanks, baby, but you forgot to kiss me. Please!' And she put those succulent lips of hers onto the reluctant mouth of the traumatised former diplomat.

Alphonsus was not in the mood, but couldn't refuse the offer, so he responded hurriedly. Then he said, 'Now you go home. I shall give you a call in the morning.'

The traditional hardliners of the party were not comfortable with the reckless outbursts of the new-age reformer, so they embarked on plans to eliminate Alphonsus Kamara. They came up with a deadly strategy.

When Alphonsus spoke to Denis, Denis told him that the hardliners were plotting to put him in hot water.

'The hardliners are not only bent on putting you out of your job, but if possible their main objective is to cook up criminal cases against you that would put you behind bars. They'll be meeting tomorrow. And you should know that your elevation to the post of Secretary General of the party was a ploy. The idea was to remove you from the Diplomatic Service and put an end to your career. Be on your guard!'

The meeting to discuss the Secretary General's downfall, and the status of diplomats in general took place at the premises of the meeting's chairman, Bonkelekeh. The stage was set. The room was colourful, befitting APC traditions and customs. In the centre was a massive table, covered with a red tablecloth bearing the image of the leader of the party, President Siato. But despite all the elegance, the proceedings were marred by chaos.

Bonkelekeh began. 'Comrades, let us pray, especially for those comrades who sacrificed their lives during the last general election. But for their dedication to the party and country we wouldn't be here today.'

According to the traditions of the party, no meeting was ever complete without the party victory song and motto being sung and shouted respectively. Thus, after the song, like hypnotised people, they repeated the party motto passionately after the chairman: 'APC, APC, now or never!' Three times, then the meeting began.

'Comrades, we all know the purpose of this meeting,' Bonkelekeh said. 'I need not waste time. I want you to put your ideas forward. One thing, we can't afford to fail!'

Then the ideas started flowing in rapidly around the table.

'I think we should literally have a grenade tied round his neck, and have him dumped into the ocean,' suggested one original thinker.

'You are quite right!' applauded another. 'He would be perfectly executed. When we came to power, they said our government was composed of a bunch of illiterates. Now that we have decided to draft the so-called educated elites and technocrats into the inner circles of our party, they are planning to overthrow us. I mean, what's wrong with Africans? We introduce controlled democracy and they shout foul! Dictatorship! What do they expect from the APC, that we bring back Christ?'

'Comrades, you forget one important thing – the craze for quick money-making. Take any diplomat who has been in the job a couple of years. What do you see? Big family cars, cars for girlfriends, fantastic houses built by the ocean in Goderich Village and, of course, fat bank accounts abroad,' said Saffa Kallon, one of the hardliners on the Central Committee.

'But how do they make all this money?' asked someone curiously.

'You tell me,' said Bonkelekeh. 'Haven't you heard of the prolific illicit smuggling rings, trading in elephant tusks, diamonds and gold? There is more to the Diplomatic Service than the narrow perception of party managers.'

'Ah! Certainly you are right Bonkelekeh,' said Saffa Kallon. 'Their greatest asset and saving grace is the diplomatic bag. Because of the diplomatic immunities that cover that bag, they can smuggle almost anything in it. Diamonds, gold, passports, you name it. That small bag conceals the dark side of our unscrupulous diplomats. They are arrogant, overconfident, full of false pride. They lack common sense.'

Haja Salaymatu nodded. 'Bonkelekeh, you must bring this issue to the attention of the Presidium at the next convention in Bo town. It is silly, isn't? We are the party managers. We work round the clock and get a lot of stick from a disgruntled electorate. And what do we get in return from our government and party? Absolutely nothing, except monthly rice quotas. Compared to what the so-called experts, educated technocrats and diplomats, especially at our foreign embassies, get, ours is a mere pittance. They receive fantastic handshakes from customers and the Presidium. These are not the values we fought for.'

'Of course, one of the values we fought for was to repay ourselves in the most corrupt manner,' whispered one of the members to a colleague.

She nodded and whispered back, 'Yes, of course, all the backhanders, sweeteners from pilgrims. Walls have ears, let's get out of here.'

They both excused themselves and went into the female toilet where they could talk freely.

'Some of these people think we are blind,' complained the first woman. 'You know, "Don't mind her, she is one of those senior politicians engaged in paying themselves in the most unscrupulous manner".'

'You don't know the half of it. A friend of mine works for Haja's organisation. Guess what? My friend told me that Haja and her Chairman have embezzled all the financial aid donated by Saudi Arabia in support of the advancement of Islam in Sierra Leone. In order to conceal and consolidate their filthy games, they have become lovers,' said the other.

Haja Salaymatu was the Chairwoman of the APC Women's League, one of the most powerful offices in the city. Also, as organiser of the APC Women's Muslim Association, her job took her to Mecca in the Holy Land during the annual pilgrimage and round the world on meetings throughout the year. Her colleagues were not impressed by her hypocritical comments about corruption in the Diplomatic Service. After all, she was also corrupt, even though she was not a diplomat. She thought people were not aware of her secret corrupt deals that did not only tarnish the good image of the party but also of the Islamic religion, of which she was a leading figure. But her opponents were afraid to attack her in the open, which was why the two ladies gossiped behind the closed doors of a female toilet.

However, one person did have the guts and the courage to criticise Haja in public. But even he was careful, and used metaphors in his sharp condemnations. That bold personality was Saffa Kallon.

Renowned for his boldness, he was nicknamed 'Ndaa Waa', which meant 'Big Mouth'. He picked his words carefully, but nevertheless rebuked Haja there and then. Like the last nail in the coffin, it threw the whole meeting into utter confusion.

'Please, Comrade Haja Salaymatu, hold your breath! You need not grumble. You upset the masses, less important people like us, when you of all people make such comments. In your case they are absolutely untrue. And you know it. You are one of the most powerful senior female officials in this party. They say those whose nuts were cracked by benevolent spirits should never forget to be humble. Not only that, those who live in glass houses should not throw stones,' said Kallon.

Haja Salaymatu bristled. 'I would expect nothing less from you Kallon. Are you not from Pendembu, one of the foremost roots of the defunct SLPP? I am not surprised at your attitude, nor should any of us round this table be. People like you and a good number of the new converts to this cause are under scrutiny. Those of us whose parents were founding members shall never lose sight of the fact that you operate on the treacherous principle of divided loyalty. Put simply, you are slippery customers, dangerous in my view, far more dangerous, than any hidden enemy.' Haja had chosen to play the divisive tribal card in order to obscure the facts and change the subject.

At this juncture the argument almost went out of control and Bonkelekeh had to intervene in order to save further deterioration of the proceedings.

'This is unlike an APC meeting. It is not part of our culture and you both know it,' he said severely. 'I must remind you that ours is a communist party. One of our core values is unity at party and individual levels; failing to adhere to this value exposes the party in general and the party leadership in particular to our enemies. Remember, the SLPP is like a sleeping lion – if you wake her up, she might stage a dramatic comeback that will hurt all of us, including members of our families. Now, for gross indiscipline and above all disrespect for my presence as your elder and chairman at this meeting the two of you must pay fines. But first of all, step forward and shake hands and let bygones be bygones.'

Haja looked at him in disbelief. 'What did you say? That, I, Haja Salaymatu of Port Lokko pay a fine for speaking the truth to a convert to the APC? No. Never. Over my dead body'. She spat on the floor in defiance. 'Let me give you a bit of a lesson on the inner secrets of this party. Hierarchies and stratas are divided into the Inherited and Bestowed layers. Mine is the first layer.' She was furious, because she had been told the naked truth and it hurt.

The meeting once again descended into acrimony, until Edith Johnson, the daughter of Sierra Leone's Consul in China, made a serious observation:

'Mr Chairman, the kind of language used in this meeting by some of my comrades is not good for the unity in our party. I must state that my comrades have negative opinions about our diplomats engaged in such difficult tasks to create a very good image of our country and party abroad. I must say that their comments are unacceptable and I shall lodge a personal complaint with our leader.' And with that she rose and departed without a backward glance.

'Oh hoo, they say when dry bones are mentioned in a proverb, the old woman becomes uneasy,' said Kallon, quoting a classic African proverb. The interpretation being that since Miss Johnson's father was a member of the Diplomatic Service, she was not only uneasy, but also extremely angered by the criticisms levied against members of that same Diplomatic Service.

Reading between the lines, Haja Salaymatu's comments and outbursts against Kallon exposed the myth of national unity that was often talked about in a state that was torn apart by corruption and nepotism.

As far as Saffa Kallon was concerned, he was angry at the hypocrisy of Alphonsus Kamara and his group of new-age reformers. As one of the hardliners of the party, Kallon's main allegation against Alphonsus in particular was that he had vaulting ambitions but masqueraded as a prudent and ardent reformer. Above all, his anger was heightened by the fact that Alphonsus had rejected the scholarship application of Josiah's nephew, Kpanabom, and Josiah was a close friend.

Saffa tried to turn the meeting back to the matter at hand – namely, Secretary General Kamara. 'His attitude has exposed his diplomatic immaturity. The problem with our diplomats is that whenever they return from overseas, the white man's land, they assume they are suddenly black Englishmen, better placed in terms of anything – knowledge, civilisation, all the ideas in this world – than anyone

32

in their own country. This man's reforms are a disgrace and he must be stopped.'

Kallon was the type of man who would never hide his true colours. Although Haja may have expressed a different opinion about him, Kallon never stabbed people in the back. He was one of the few brave and outspoken members of a party that discouraged variety in terms of political opinions.

At its dictatorial best, the APC deemed every supporter a mere political tool designed for a particular objective – the advancement of the aspirations of the party. In the process, all were bound to answer 'yes sir' to the party hierarchies. Sit down, yes sir, stand up, yes sir, yes sir and yes sir. Even members of the Central Committee danced to this tune. They were political tools, puppets, they were there to be seen but not heard. This philosophy underpinned the core values of the APC and was imposed on the masses as well.

But, Kallon was not a mere tool. Although he was vocal about the inculcation of ethical values into party politics, he was markedly different from most of his colleagues in the sense that he would do nothing clandestine to undermine the general credibility or the political stability of the party. He was a party loyalist, but with a difference. His colleagues often referred to him as a gentleman politician and a straight loyalist.

In fact he made every effort to win more souls from among his own ethnic group, the Mendes, to the APC cause, irrespective of the general ill-feelings that vibrated throughout the length and breadth of the eastern province when the SLPP fell from grace. Perhaps his only crime was that he was not often as economical with the truth as most of his colleagues.

'I am not an idealist, but a prudent and ardent realist,' he often lashed out at his critics.

For instance, he was on record as having publicly told President Siato at a party convention that no matter how popular the party was, nor how tightly it held onto power, it was a transient thing. All political party's were thus. These were the comments of a political realist, not an empty idealist.

But, sadly, the model of communism that was propounded by a handful of people in the party like Kallon was not an attractive proposition for the top echelons. The style of communism that they preached was big on ideology and very short on useful reality.

5

Pen vs Sword

Saffa Kallon and Uncle Josiah were not only political allies under the banner of the APC; they had both served as underdogs in the Sierra Leone army. They had also worked intermittently in the same regiment at the Moa Barracks, Daru.

During those immensely difficult days they made tremendous sacrifices and covered one another's backs when it was necessary. They had common enemies and friends. This was during the era of the British Empire, so discipline in the army was at its highest level. Worst of all, black officers were at the receiving end of inherent iniquities. But they managed to transcend it all and survive. Their relationship endured because of a common philosophy on life: the philosophy of 'watch my back as I watch yours, and let my friend be your friend, and your enemy, be my enemy'.

So for Saffa Kallon to stand by and watch Alphonsus the impostor ruin the prospects of his comrade's nephew, Kpanabom, was just an unthinkable thing. He would join forces with anyone in order to help Josiah engineer the demise of the common enemy, Alphonsus. But it was a far-fetched dream. In fact, the first attempt was counterproductive in a dramatic way.

There is a saying that walls have ears. Similarly, rumour, we are told, has a million tongues and interpretations, and they were soon at work, wagging out the news of the failed meeting held by the hardliners to 'finish off' Alphonsus, the loathsome Secretary General. Although each tongue told a different story, the essential facts tallied.

Eventually, the secret meeting was leaked to the public domain by a tabloid newspaper, in the most dramatic fashion. The effects immediately shook the fabric of security in the diplomatic circles of Moscow and Freetown. The million-dollar question was: who leaked this information and why was a simple newspaper headline misread and misconstrued by diplomats as well as politicians?

When the APC came to power, like all political parties in Africa, they effectively dismantled freedom of expression, including the free press. All opposition newspapers were banned, save the government newspapers *We Yone* and *The Daily Mail.* All but one: the new government spared a two-page tabloid operated by journalists who had just completed their studies at Fourah Bay College. This was *The Tablet.* It was a combination of token appeasement and the fact that a blood relative, uncle of the editor, Peter Furnell was a senior minister in the APC government. he may have influenced the decision.

As former proactive Students' Union leaders and journalists, the editor and writers brought these values to bear on mainstream politics and journalism, which impacted enormously on *The Tablet*'s readers throughout the land. These proactive values were simple but ideal for a nation that was vulnerable to unscrupulous and unpatriotic politicians. The values were courage, vibrancy and radicalism in exposing corruption in society, no matter what the cost.

The young journalists working on the paper believed

that the most worthy service a man or woman could offer was to die for the cause of justice and the love of one's country.

Though the quality of the paper was not that good, it had two advantages. First, it was the only free paper left in the country; and second, it commanded the support of the young and the disgruntled working-class masses.

In essence, *The Tablet* served as the conscience of the downtrodden people, including students, in Siato's Sierra Leone.

It was to this vibrant and radical channel that the mole from the meeting leaked the news of its occurrence and its failure in relation to the elimination of Alphonsus Kamara. The next day, the paper carried a controversial article, the bold headline of which captivated the attention of many readers in Freetown and beyond. Most importantly, it set diplomatic and political flames alight. The consequences were severe for the regime.

The explosive headline read:

SIATO REGIME FACES CRISIS AS APC OFFICIALS CONSPIRE TO REMOVE SECRETARY GENERAL

The APC had been in power a long time. A virtual police state, the country was run on the basis of everyone spying on everyone else. There was of course a formidable national security network, controlled by three key figures. Each had a special code name and telephone number. Only President Siato was privy to their particulars. The Special Branch classified them as highly sensitive state secrets.

Who were they? Their titles were the Force Commander (code named Tiger), the Commissioner of Police (code named Sniffer) and the Head of the Secret Service or

Special Branch (code named Cobra). Of the three, Cobra was the most devoted and seasoned officer. He took his work so seriously that it overtook his love and care of his family. He was a workaholic, who toiled round the clock. He had a special room in his house, code named 'Dungeon'. It was here that he performed emergency and unfinished jobs after official working hours.

He was a typical Cold War spy, and no double agent. Most importantly, he was an unshakable party loyalist, a die-hard according to political analysts. Cobra distinguished himself professionally by undergoing various training courses. They included logistics, strategy and espionage in British, Russian and Nigerian military and spy academies.

Very early in the morning, before *The Tablet* had been circulated on the streets of Freetown, someone informed Sniffer, who in turn relayed the message to Cobra about the awful front cover bombshell. Sniffer emphasised that they had to act with the utmost urgency in order to avoid serious trouble for national security.

'By six-thirty this morning, *The Tablet* boys will set this whole nation alight. We must act now, else . . .'

'Let's meet at your office in five minutes,' Cobra suggested.

Cobra was still in his pyjamas. While he struggled to get dressed as quickly as he could, the fax machine in the Dungeon spewed out highly sensitive messages which also needed his attention. His wife Miranda, used to such early starts and sudden emergencies, had risen calmly and was brewing tea in the kitchen.

Unfortunately, her husband would have no time to drink it. He was beset with the most important affairs of state, much more important than a cup of tea. In frustration, he tore at the buttons of his pyjamas and pulled on his clothes.

Seeing his urgency, Miranda gave up on offering him any tea. She knew he wouldn't drink it.

Cobra drove quickly, and in less than two minutes he arrived at the office of the Commissioner of Police, in George Street, opposite the National Treasury buildings.

Sniffer greeted him. 'Ah, old soldier, you are fast and in good shape. Let's get down to business straight away.' He spread out the early edition of *The Tablet* on the round table, and drew Cobra's attention to the headline. 'Look at what *The Tablet* has done,' he said disgustedly.

'What action do you want us to take?' the chief spy asked calmly.

Sniffer's table was awash with trays of internal and external memos, six telephones, three fax machines and one VHF set. The telephones and VHF set linked him directly to the President, the Vice Presidents, Cabinet Ministers, all police Commanders, the Chief of the army and the Director of Prisons.

Desperately, he reached for his gold-plated cigarette case and lit up with a gold-plated cigarette lighter. The huge pressure that went with his job had turned him into a chain-smoker. Three decades of heavy smoking had been supplemented by large amounts of whisky, and his health was not good. Many of his critics called him 'the living dead'.

'It's a matter of national security. What we do is up to you.'

Cobra knew when a buck was being passed. He too reached for a cigarette and lit up.

'Indeed sir, but my department answers directly to you, so I need to know your own opinions before I act,' he countered.

In truth, Cobra had no real idea of what they could do. Stop the paper being distributed? Surely impossible in the time. Both men were at a loss, and their jobs were on the line.

As they stood there, undecided, two daily incident reports were handed to Sniffer. Both were coded urgent. He glanced at them.

(A) 2 senior police officers caught with 10 carats of diamonds in Yengema, Kono District. They are remanded in custody, awaiting your instructions, sir. Signed Fineth Johnson, Chief Police Officer, Kono District.

(B) 3 prostitutes killed overnight at the Longsteps and Kartarkummbay brothels. Suspects are 1 military officer, 1 Police Officer (ISU DIV) and 12 Executive Officers. All in police cells. Signed Alpha Koroma, CPO, Crime, Central Police Station.

As he read, one of his fax machines discharged another message:

Guerrilla warfare broken out in Pujehun District.
The leaders call themselves Ndoh gbo wusue.
Signed Shaku Konneh, O/C Pujehun District.

Sniffer sighed and looked wearily at Cobra. 'Police officers in custody for diamond smuggling and murder, and *The Tablet* about to turn the city upside down – what a job!'

Finally he made up his mind and decided that they should inform Tiger, the Force Commander. As he reached for the receiver in order to call Tiger, the green phone rang. It was the Foreign Office.

'Good morning sir, please hold on for the Foreign Minister,' came the voice of Yamiday, the Minister's Private Secretary.

Now Sniffer was trembling. They had delayed too long. Copies of the paper were on the streets. In fact, the Foreign Minister had a copy in front of him as they spoke.

No sooner had that awful call ended, another came in. This time it was the Special Branch officer attached to the Waterloo District, one of the outskirts of Freetown. In a trembling voice he said: 'Sir, *The Tablet* has caused mayhem here. It's out on the streets and in all the classrooms of the Waterloo school. People are scrambling to buy copies, sir.'

While this call was being made, a small-time trader who sold cassava bread and fried fish for a living arrived to collect payment for the regular supplies of the same from the Special Branch officer, Sub-Inspector, Thomas Jackson. She was a nineteen-year-old graduate from the Peninsular Secondary School, Waterloo. With three General Certificate examination passes in Bible knowledge, government studies and economics, Aminata Johnson was now out on the streets of Waterloo, jobless, and fending for a living. It had been three years since she had left school.

'I have come to collect my cash,' she said.

The officer was so furious that he retorted: 'Cash? Cash! Look, girl, there's serious trouble happening, and you're talking about inconsequential things like cash!'

Waterloo, like most other suburban areas in Sierra Leone, was impoverished and suffered from chronic under-development. The unemployment rate was at its highest ever and deprivation was rife and spreading. The only local industry was fishing, and it was at subsistence level.

Most worrying about Waterloo was the fact that past

elections and political trends had shown that it was not an entirely APC stronghold. Thus, the authorities always felt that Waterloo could be a loose cannon, ready to explode at the slightest opportunity. So, when it was learned that *The Tablet* had reached Waterloo, there was an alarming feeling that it could trigger an uprising against the regime.

Panic began to set in.

Cobra's office was completely inundated and the pressure kept building up. The entire nation was now in the grip of the news.

The Sierra Leone Ambassador in Moscow now informed President Siato by telephone. This strange method of communicating the news to the President came about in this way. When intelligence about the article was faxed to Moscow by the Russian Ambassador in Freetown, his counterpart in Moscow was summoned at 7.30 a.m. to the Foreign Office. From there he was whisked off to the Politbureau, and then brought back to the Foreign Office at 10 a.m. There and then, against all diplomatic principles and ethics, he was pressurised by the Russian Foreign Minister into calling President Siato at the State House in Freetown, to 'clear the air'.

As the papers were being sold in their thousands on the streets of Freetown, news about the pending diplomatic roars that the headline had generated between Sierra Leone and the USSR spread like a bushfire. It was amazing that a tiny tabloid of little or no significance in a little-known Third World state had virtually shaken the fabric of one of the two major superpowers: the USSR.

But no one doubted what was at stake. Senior heads would roll, diplomatic relations would be strained, and the crisis could easily extend beyond the shores of Sierra Leone and Moscow. The entire episode lent credence to the adage that 'the pen is mightier than the sword'.

42

6

Meeting of the Presidium

One of the key trademarks of the police state that obtained in President Siato's Sierra Leone was the absolute centralisation of decision-making powers. This culture affected all state apparatuses. For example, promotions in the armed forces including the police had to receive the scrutiny and blessing of the State House. Since the last general election in 1988, promotions of the top cadres of the police, the prison service, the Internal Security Unit and the army had been put on hold. However, the sticky point was that while it was possible for the regime to postpone indefinitely or put on hold the promotions of many sectors of the armed forces, there were exceptions to this rule: the army, the Internal Security Unit and the police were like untouchables. The reason was simple: in a dictatorship such as Sierra Leone these three wings of the armed forces were the nerve-centre of the kind of national security that was required to guarantee the survival and stability of the regime.

It was a serious situation. In fact, gossips had it that certain disgruntled elements in the army were contemplating a *coup d'état* because of unsatisfactory conditions, such as delayed promotions and poor salaries.

It has to be said that the regime always accorded the

armed forces preferential treatment. For instance, the senior cadres in particular enjoyed frivolous material and financial incentives such as monthly rice quotas and salary bonuses each time they rigged elections, which no other sector of society was ever accorded. Now, it seemed, even this might not be enough.

Despite its ownership of deposits of natural resources including diamonds and gold, and the proceeds from cash crops, the poor global economic performance of the late 1970s had corresponding effects on the economic performance of Sierra Leone. This was compounded by the fact that the regime suffered from gross financial indiscipline.

For instance, misappropriation of government funds by the top brass of the regime led to huge foreign debts, scarcity of foreign exchange and the imposition of severe IMF World Bank structural adjustment conditions and policy on an already impoverished nation. These conditions and policy were not economically sound. They were unrealistic as they brought no economic renewal or recovery, but abject poverty and social unrests. It spelt out the preconditions for IMF World Bank loans to third world countries, such as cuts on petrol and rice subsidies.

In the past however, when the regime suffered from similar problems, it had respite in the form of foreign aid. The USSR was a generous donor, but the publication of the infamous article in *The Tablet* was set to throw the prospects of any external financial bailouts from Moscow into serious jeopardy.

Regardless, the regime had to find ways and means of redressing the promotion problem at all costs; otherwise it risked being wrong-footed by the top brass of the army. Therefore, the triumvirate of the Father, Son and Holy

Ghost held an emergency meeting of the Presidium at the State House in Freetown.

The State House is the official residence of the President. It is a massive complex, built by the British colonial administration on the top of Tower Hill. During colonial days, it served as the official residence of Governor-Generals. The State House has many rumours and mysteries attached to its history. Some say that there is an underground tunnel running from it all the way to the sea at Deep Water Quay, an escape route for any Governor-General in case of crisis. This is probably true, and if so was certainly prudent, for the British administration was never popular, and gave rise to much conflict, such as the war over the British 'Hut Tax', waged by Chief Bai Bureh.

Such stories aside, the State House is a historic colonial landmark, and has always been a symbol of power. Decisions governing life and death are taken within the confines of this massive edifice. And it still maintains this importance, for since political independence the State House has served as the official residence of all heads of state, including democrats, conservatives, whisky socialists, military captains, dictators and rouged regimes. So it was appropriate that the promotion crisis meeting was held at the State House.

It was apparent that nothing, absolutely nothing, would stand in the way of President Siato in seeing to it that his top cadres were promoted.

Whether it meant starving the poor, whether they died from disease or not, whether the city slumbered in continuous blackouts or not, whether the youths, graduates and school leavers remained jobless or not, whether teachers abandoned classrooms because of unpaid salaries or not, the regime must make room for promotions in the armed forces. It had done worse and survived. It would do this, and survive.

The two Vice Presidents were off to the meeting. They rode in a complex and huge entourage of private and official security motorcades. Among the many vehicles were six Mercedes state cars and six Land Rovers. The cost of running and keeping these cars would have paid off the salary arrears of 70 per cent of the nation's civil servants and teachers put together for six months. It was yet another example of the socioeconomic malaise that gripped the country.

The motorcades arrived at the State House at 1 p.m. The First Vice President emerged from his car, surrounded by bodyguards, with their AK47s and pistols at the ready to shoot at and kill without hesitation any person deemed to be a threat to security. The Vice President was dressed in an immaculate long white gown, which suited his lanky build. After the cameras and pressmen had taken their shots, he went through the first chains of security checks in the basement. Then out came the Second Vice President, dressed in a khaki safari suit. He was of medium height with the calm eyes of a meditator. He was also led through the security doors after the necessary security checks. Then, both men waited in the cabinet waiting room on the ground floor.

While they waited, the First Vice President reflected sadly on the hundreds of letters written by his constituents asking for financial help. Some of them had spent days without food; others had had their children thrown out of school for lack of fees. Every day letters and messages from hundreds of beggars landed on his desk. Sadly, only 2 per cent ever had favourable responses. More often than not the letters were relegated to the waste paper basket.

The entourage was now given the green light to commence the second phase of their journey upstairs. They went through another set of stringent security checks. When they got to the third checkpoint, one of the senior police officers, a distant relative of the girlfriend of the First Vice President, came to attention, saluted him and whispered, 'I implore you to protect my interests sir.' He was reminding the Vice President not to forget to push the case for his promotion.

They proceeded up a long carpeted flight of stairs into a large lofty room on the fifth floor, where they were escorted into the office of the President. They took their seats and waited for his arrival.

As usual, the meeting commenced by singing the party victory song, followed by shouting the party slogan three times.

Then the President spoke. 'You are summoned here comrades to discuss the promotions of our great men and women in uniform.'

The President's secretary consulted the huge service files at his side and pulled out documents relating to various personnel. The team then went through them, one by one, to emphasise the meticulous nature of the regime.

Slowly they proceeded through the files, until they arrived at the critical promotion: the post of Deputy Brigadier, or Force Commander. At this point the President took absolute command of the meeting. Only he could decide anything relating to this vital post, as he was the Commander of the armed forces, and without peer.

The President looked at his two Vice Presidents as if daring them to speak, and cleared his throat. 'Criteria for promotion to the rank of Deputy Brigadier, comrades, no comments!' Like robots, they simply nodded their heads in humble approval. The president appended his signature and presidential seal to the promotion of one Jack Saidu Martin, nicknamed 'Josephine Talker', meaning a weak, indecisive chatterer. And indeed 'Josephine Talker' led a weak, deplorable government when he succeeded president Siato on 1 October 1985.

All the spin put aside, the procedure was extremely flawed on several counts. Prior to the meeting of the Presidium, the triumvirs had had shared access to a comprehensive list of the potential candidates and kept a copy each. At this meeting, they were only supposed to discuss whether the candidates put forward for promotion met the 'necessary criteria'. Which begged the serious question: who compiled the lists of criteria and competences? Of course, as commanding officers, they were responsible, nominally at least, for promoting or otherwise the men and women under their command. Thus, this meeting of the Presidium was in reality not much more than a rubber-stamping exercise.

The infamous phrase 'necessary criteria' associated with promotions was nothing other than a political gimmick. It was fluid and politically deceptive. It meant different things to different people, for Sierra Leoneans were aware of the fact that promotions in the armed forces were informed by bribery, corruption and regional and tribal affiliation, not prudence or as a reflection of competence or dedication. Such a policy undermined morale in the force, but unfortunately was at the heart of the policies of the regime.

At this meeting the Presidium endorsed all the candidates for promotion with the exception of two senior police officers. They were the Chief Superintendents, Momoh Jusu and Alimammy Kamara, both from the central police station at King Jimmy, the divisional headquarters in Freetown.

'Why do you think we should promote these two odd officers?' the President asked curiously after he had signed all the other promotions without complaint.

'They have met the necessary criteria, Mr President,' replied, the First Vice President.

'And what do you say, Second Vice President?' the President asked. He buzzed for his aide-de-camp and asked for something called the 'SS File'. This was a Secret Service file that contained sensitive top-secret information regarding senior members of the armed forces, such as their political activities and affiliations – anything in fact that might cast doubt on their allegiance to the APC regime.

The President opened the file and read out the Special Branch reports on the general conduct of the officers. Cobra had compiled them. The main charge against the two men was political disloyalty. It seemed that they had supported the United Democratic Party of Dr Smith at the first general election in the long brutal history of the APC regime. At that time, the two officers were attached to the Special Branch and were working directly under the supervision of Cobra.

The President shook his head. 'We cannot promote these men. I'm amazed they're on the list at all. They are not, in my opinion, to be trusted.'

'So what do we do next, Father of the Nation?' asked the First Vice President.

'A good question, Mr First Vice President. Not only am I going to refuse their promotion, I think it wise to force their retirement immediately.'

He called in his secretary and dictated a short memo to Sniffer. 'The following officers are to be retired from the service with effect from today, noontime. They are Chief Superintendents Momoh Jusu and Alimammy Kamara.' He applied the seal of office to the document and signed it at once. The presidential ink was green, which distinguished it from all other signatures in the land.

Now the meeting turned its attention to the article in *The Tablet*, but as they were about to begin their discussion the high priority phone, painted in the national colours of Sierra Leone – green, white and blue – rang.

President Siato was a very tall man, a giant figure with an imposing personality. His health was failing, and nowadays he had to be helped out of his chair and his physical activity was limited. Sometimes he even had trouble speaking when he was sitting down. Some believed that his condition was due to the thousands of speeches he had delivered, all standing up, when in his younger days he had been active in the Trade Union movement.

Assisted by his ADC, President Siato took up the receiver. 'Yes?'

The line was bad and the voice was faint. 'Mr President, Moscow here . . .'

Then he could hear nothing but static. His anger, which had been building for the last few seconds and was never slow to erupt, boiled over. Had he not expressly asked that the problem with the line be fixed immediately? Did these people think he used the presidential hotline to talk to his mother?

'Why is this problem with the line not fixed?' he bellowed, suddenly seized with a frightening degree of vitality. 'You!' He pointed at his quivering ADC, 'Did I not expressly ask for this problem to be fixed?'

'Yes, your Excellency, and I . . .'

But he was not allowed to finish.

'And you!' bellowed the President, staring at the First Vice President, 'You are responsible too! Don't you care whether we can communicate with other countries in a crisis?'

'Yes sir, of course but . . .'

The President cut him off, launching into a tirade of abuse. Such rants were legendary, and all the men present knew there was nothing they could do but sit it out until the storm blew over. This was what was known throughout the nation as 'Siato Fever'.

This particular rage lasted nearly fifteen minutes, covering a wide range of sins and failings on the part of his deputies. They found it amazing that a man so apparently feeble could summon up the energy. Surely, they believed, it would be a temper tantrum, not an assassin's bullet, that would carry the President to his maker.

When he finally ran out of steam, President Siato ordered his smarting underlings to take him back to his golden chair, at which point the telephone rang again. The Vice Presidents quailed. The President frowned at the phone, then answered it.

'Siato, speaking.'

This time the President could hear perfectly well, but the caller only said three words. Then the line went dead, and the President paled.

The words were: 'All financial support . . .'

What did it mean? Was all financial aid being withdrawn? Siato trembled. He had recognised the voice, and it was no underling relaying a message, but the messenger himself: the leader of the Politbureau.

The President pulled himself together. He must not, must *never* show weakness in front of his inferiors. He had no intention of revealing to them what he had just heard;

not yet anyway. They were political wolves, he knew, and they would not hesitate to take any chance to oust him from power and fill the golden chair themselves.

The President brought the meeting to an abrupt halt. He was extremely angry and frustrated. His Vice Presidents left in a state of uncertainty due to the fact that their President refused to tell them what he had heard on the phone that had seemed to shake him so.

'The line must have gone dead,' said the First Vice President as they left the building.

'Yes, but who was it, and what did they say to make old Siato go so pale?' said his colleague.

He thought he could guess.

7

Money Talks

The party hardliners had not given up on their plans to eliminate Kamara, but their schemes were now doomed to failure. They were now on a collision course with the free press, in the form of *The Tablet* and did they but know it, with the President himself.

Two things helped to exacerbate this situation. First, two letters were written by Edith Johnson and Saffa Kallon to President Siato. They were followed by a leak from the Party Secretariat to the effect that Uncle Josiah had bribed one of the secretaries on the scholarship board in order to reinstate the name of his nephew on the final list.

The Johnson family was fortunate in the sense that they had money and wielded influence in political circles. They owed their wealth to Grandpa Johnson, as he was fondly known, but his full baptismal and a confirmation name was Horitio Matia Gigba Johnson. Born in Mano Dasse in the southern province around 1908, he amassed wealth and influence through greedy commercial pursuits in fishing, coffee and the ginger trade along the Tabe, Gboodape, Moa and Sherbro Rivers. His business tactics were ruthlessly selfish and greedy. He squeezed wealth particularly out of impoverished illiterate locals. He would exchange items such as bead, salt, clothes, tobacco, rum and sugar for the hard earned commodities of the local people. Sometimes he would pay peanuts for them or push the financially desperate ones to the wall and force them to borrow money from him. In that case they would pay very high rates of interest for many years. As he was one of the few people in the district at that time who could read and write, he also acted as an interpreter and mediator between foreign and local businesses. Close to the declaration of independence, he transferred his business empire to Freetown and served as a middleman, a broker between the white commercial elite and the local people. All of these roles served his commercial interests. By the time of independence, he had numerous properties in Freetown, Bo, Makeni, Moyamba, Dasse, Pendembu, Segbwema and Daru. He gave his only son, Edith's father Conelius Johnson, a decent education and the rights of inheritance, and introduced him to the rich and powerful throughout the land. In this way he secured a career in the Diplomatic Service.

In 1968 Grandpa Johnson died peacefully in his sleep, leaving his massive fortune to his son Cornilius and his granddaughter Edith. Cornilius made the most of his good fortune. First he gave his only child and daughter, Edith, a decent education and acquired for her a top job in the Sierra Leone Civil Service.

Edith worked as an Assistant Secretary in the Cabinet Office. Wasting no time, she took full advantage of her beauty and social status. First, she fell in love with her boss, the Secretary to the Cabinet, Theophilus Adebayoh Smith, and then with the President himself. Both these liaisons helped to cushion her position and that of her father. Her beauty and high-class qualities dazzled President Siato so much that she gained command of the President's heart. Thus, in no time, he elevated her to the status of senior concubine.

Three weeks after the disastrous meeting concerning the fate of Alphonsus Kamara, she contacted her father in China, and he agreed that she should write to the President voicing her concerns following the meeting. The letter was brief and to the point. And as one would expect, by virtue of their relationship, the contents and language were far from official. In brief, it was a letter that dealt with serious matters of state, but it was punctuated by romantic language and sentiments. It read:

Your Excellency,

It's months now since I had my last quota (laugh)! Whoever may have occupied your time must be under the delusion that she has won a permanent place in your heart.

But you and I are aware that I have a special place in your heart, which no one, not even the Queen of Sheba, would succeed in claiming. Darling, I promise you a double quality performance and revenge with impunity when we meet before my birthday falls. Forget not, I am the one and only senior concubine in our infinite world of romance that we so romantically enjoy!

On a serious note, I wonder whether you are aware of a meeting held at Chief Bonkelekeh's premises three weeks ago? If my recollections are right, I think that he and his cronies have skeletons in their cupboards. The meeting was informed by serious rebellious undertones.

Sweetie, please be careful and remember your political philosophy – unlike in the army, there is no brother in politics!

Everything is kept intact for your Excellency.

Agape always,

Omo

When Miss Johnson finished the letter she let one of her trusted juniors, Ema Goba, proofread it. It was a sad mistake, for she was not aware that both of them were rivals over the Cabinet Secretary. Ema praised the contents of the letter. Omo smiled.

'Well, Sierra Leoneans have always looked down on the President because he is not a university graduate. But what they have failed to recognise is that he has excellent communication and people skills. His powers of oratory, presentation and writing are exemplary. These qualities have made him the wonderful and successful President he is. Yes, university qualification is unique, you can't underestimate that, otherwise our parents wouldn't have gone all out to educate us to university level. His Excellency is a superb letter writer, a skill he gained at the Ruskin College in the UK when he was a student. I'll tell you for free that my sweetie recognises and enjoys quality writing.

'Surely, that was why he fell for you, Omo, because you're also a good writer. They say birds of the same feather flock together.'

Omo grinned. 'Come on, you cheeky little thing, let me have the letter and get back to your work.' She patted Ema on the back as a sign of appreciation for proofreading her masterpiece.

During the lunch break, Edith went to the State House and gave the letter to the President's ADC. He was the only person at the State House who was privy to their relationship. The letter reached Siato that same day, in the evening as he was accepting the credentials of the New Guinean Ambassador to Sierra Leone, H.E. Momodou Keita.

When the ADC entered the office, the ceremony was at its height. It lasted for two hours. After everyone had left he saluted and handed over the envelope. There was no need to ponder over the sender, for the President recognised the handwriting immediately. He smiled and opened the letter, curtly dismissing the ADC from his presence.

He had hardly finished reading Omo's letter when another one landed on his desk. This time it was a complaint letter written by Saffa Kallon. In it he catalogued the proceedings of the abortive meeting at Chief Bonkelekeh's.

In the third paragraph, he wrote:

I come from the eastern region of this country where our party has not yet gained firm roots, except for Kono, in the diamond fields. We therefore need to raise the profile of the party in that region, but I do not believe that this will be possible if it is widely known that a relative of a senior party official has been refused official privileges.

The final paragraph referred to the dubious activities of senior diplomats in the party:

I crave your indulgence to reflect carefully on one salient point – if diplomats abroad are using our nation's diplomatic bags in order to enrich themselves, their families and friends, then we had better dismantle our embassies or withdraw those who carry these bags.

A week and half passed, and Kallon received no response from the State House. One evening, Kallon phoned Uncle Josiah and proposed a visit to Fullah Town, in Freetown.

'One of my fiancées lives there, and I could, as it were, kill two birds with one stone.'

Uncle Josiah smiled and ribbed his old friend. 'Fiancée, eh? And how many of those do you have just now, at your tender age of fifty something?'

'Age has nothing to do with it Josiah! I am still fit enough to father a child, should I so wish.'

Josiah laughed. 'Oh, I didn't mean to question your sexual prowess my friend. I was just wondering if such liaisons might not be, well, a threat to your position.'

'No, no. You forget, I am an African and a Muslim. I may have more than one wife.'

'Now how could I have forgotten that?' Josiah said sardonically. 'See you there then.'

Prior to the visit Kallon had asked his fiancée, Elimina Tejan Cole, to secure the Russian scholarship for Kpanabom. She agreed on condition that they bribe one of the secretaries at the party Secretariat. He told her that on no account should Josiah hear of the arrangement. He wanted to surprise him.

So they arrived at the house of Elimina Cole and struck the deal that evening. They gave her five hundred leones, to be handed to Miss Elizabeth Kowa, a Senior Executive Officer and Scholarship Board member. She would now ensure that Kpanabom's name was on the final list.

'There will be no problems,' Elimina assured her visitors. 'Elizabeth is virtually in overall command of the awards. She is . . . flexible in her approach, and she makes a nice profit out of scholarship deals every year.'

Elizabeth Kowa did indeed have the whole business sewn up to her advantage. But she was careful not to associate herself too closely with the corruption. She had a negotiator, one Pa Sorie Conteh, who met the 'customers' and dealt with the paperwork. He was a senior member of the League of Chief Messengers, comprising Chief Messengers of all the ministries, including State House.

These people were not just ordinary messengers. They were highly trusted individuals, privy to some of the innermost secrets of the government, and they had been serving their country for many years. They were regarded as trustworthy. But as with any organisation, the League of Chief Messengers had its rotten elements, people who abused their position for personal gain. They leaked government information to members of the public, they engaged in all manner of corruption. Pa Sorie Conteh was a classic example of this breed.

What he and Elizabeth Kowa did not know was that Pa Sorie had become careless. He was a drunkard, and when drunk he let his tongue run away with him. He was indiscreet. And his treachery had been noticed.

The result was that this particular little deal was soon to be public knowledge, courtesy of a leak to *The Tablet*. Sure enough, the next day *The Tablet* carried another eye-catching headline:

POLITICAL TRAVESTY!
SENIOR APC COMMITTEE MEMBERS BRIBE FOR
RUSSIAN SCHOLARSHIP

The paper sold almost half a million copies throughout the land, bringing more unwelcome pressure on the regime.

In the midst of all this upheaval loomed the prospect of

the next party convention, scheduled to take place at Bo Kakowa. This was not one of the party's strongholds, which was why it had been chosen. There was little point in promoting the party in areas where support for it was strong.

8

The Conflict Intensifies

Bo Kakowa was fondly known as 'Sweet Bo' during the heyday days of Sierra Leone. It was the second largest town to Freetown in importance, though in fact a much larger place. Residents regarded their town not as a town but as a city, as equally important as Freetown, though of course in reality this was not so. Only Freetown held official city status.

The two main political parties, the SLPP and the APC, divided political allegiance, support and loyalty along regional tribal boundaries. So, the APC, being a northern party, maintained strong support in the North, while the SLPP had her political base in the South and the East. Bo Kakowa, being the provincial capital of the South, was the home of the SLPP. The West of the country tended to be regarded as 'neutral': that is to say, full of floating voters.

The advent of one-party politics in Sierra Leone brought with it the inevitable propaganda that there was only one party, and no opposition. This of course was not true, and both the people and the politicians knew it. It was, however, the official line, and had to be abided by, in public at any rate.

The truth was that the green palm tree, which was the symbol of the SLPP, was now greener than ever before, while the red sun of the APC remained a vibrant symbol of the future for that party's supporters. The country remained politically divided, one-party rule or not.

President Siato knew all of this. He knew that the SLPP were a potent force, and he knew that they must be undermined at all costs. He also knew that Bo Kakowa was a hotbed of SLPP hardliners, and believed that a party convention there would confound them and discourage revolutionary mutterings.

Alphonsus Kamara neither supported the APC nor the defunct SLPP. Yes he served the APC, but in this he had no choice. Like most educated men in Sierra Leone he was a product of history. However, he was also a new-age reformer through and through, which, as we know, put him in direct conflict with the hardliners in the APC.

As soon as Alphonsus discovered that there was a plot to bring him down, he did not, as many might have expected, kow-tow to the regime. Instead he returned to Freetown and began to consolidate his ties with fellow liberals and reformers. Recent revelations in *The Tablet* had revealed that paper to be a powerful tool in his fight against tyranny, and he vowed to make the best possible use he could of the tiny paper with its countrywide influence.

Denis Dickson, Alphonsus' close friend and confidante, suggested that the Secretary General should meet with representatives from the paper as soon as possible. And he suggested that the meeting place be Bo Kakowa.

Alphonsus asked him why there. What he actually said was, 'Why Bo town?'

'Bo town! You know that Bo is not a town, it is a city! A heroic city!'

'Oh dear, you Mende boys. So sensitive about dear old Bo!' said Alphonsus. 'You know as well as I that Sierra Leone has only one city, and that is Freetown. To have more than one city risks fragmentation of power and government. And after all, we hardly need two cities do we? The country has only a population of some three million people. Heavens, our country is corrupt enough without another administrative centre to corrupt it even more!'

Denis shook his head. 'Alphonsus, Bo deserves city status for many reasons. It hosts the best educational institutions, in particular the "mighty" Bo School, the land around is rich in natural resources and more people live there than in Freetown.'

'Come on Denis, be realistic. Don't you see that all making Bo a city would do would be to encourage split allegiances? Maybe, at worst, civil war? Anyway, Bo School, though good, is not the only school of quality in the land. It's just that you people think it is, because it's in your area! There are others equally good.'

Denis struggled not to smile as he said stubbornly, 'Name them!'

'All right! The Prince of Wales Grammar School, St Francis, Makeni, the only school of languages in the country, Anne Walsh, the Kenema Government School, the Albert Academy . . . the list is endless.'

Denis finally admitted defeat. 'All right, all right! Let us stop before things become too childish. Back to business. When you come to the meeting, I want you to bring any evidence you gathered of corrupt practice when you were in Moscow. The representatives of *The Tablet* will be most interested in anything you can show them. They want to make a tangible case supported by substantial documentary evidence. That first headline had a huge impact but the article itself was short on substance. From now on we need to try and hit the regime with solid, supportable facts. The spirits of our ancestors are on our side Alphonsus! We have the opportunity to really put the government on the ropes. We must take our chances and act now; else we are doomed to damnation. Remember the incident at Gingerhall, Alphonsus! It is still fresh in the memories of this traumatised nation, even thought it was nearly ten years ago. Babies, children, women, the aged, were all burnt to ashes. Why? To maintain the status quo. It is incumbent on you and I to crush that status quo, not with a dagger, like they do, but with the might of the pen. The pen is mightier than the sword. No throne, no principality has ever defied that logic. But I stress again, we must tighten all the loopholes, as any slips could lead to our downfall and not theirs.'

'I know what you're saying Denis. I can feel the weight of our responsibility. I promise, and swear on my first Holy Communion as a Catholic, that we shall not fail. I am compiling all the evidence as we speak. I know for sure that the pile in my possession is a millstone. Put around their necks, the culprits won't escape. But I must confess that I owe all the ideas to outwit this regime and its hardliners to no other person but you, my dear friend Denis.'

Alphonsus felt tears coming to his eyes, and he quickly concluded their conversation. The die was cast.

When the group comprising the editor of *The Tablet*, Peter Fornell, their freelance reporter, Fallah Buedu, Alphonsus Kamara and Denis Dickson arrived in Bo Kakowa, they convened the meeting at the Mugomeh, a local bar. People from all walks of like met here, especially at weekends, to socialise, gather and share information. It had been one of the most popular social venues in Bo Kakowa, during the swinging days.

Alphonsus brought a catalogue of documentary evidence to the meeting. In order to be on the safe side, he and Denis stated firmly that their names must remain anonymous. The evidence Alphonsus presented to the group was staggering, not least the paperwork that proved the sale of diplomatic and service passports to smugglers of elephant tusks, diamonds and gold, and drug traffickers.

The smugglers, mostly Lebanese nationals, middle-ranking party officials and indigenous capitalist businessmen and women, constituted a formidable ring. They were a cartel with political backing and economic strength. They connived with diplomats, ministers and senior party officials at the party Secretariat in Freetown. They used the official diplomatic bags in order to enjoy diplomatic immunity at police and immigration checkpoints. Sierra Leone embassies and consulates in Liberia, Germany, the USSR, China, Nigeria and Ghana were involved in the cartel of smuggling that robbed the Sierra Leonean taxpayers of tens of millions of leones, the equivalent of millions American dollars; money that would have built modern hospitals, schools and colleges, and financed a modern, quality police force.

With the weight of evidence so great, it was agreed at the end of the meeting that Fallah Buedu should embark on investigative journalism and do some undercover work in Monrovia and Guinea, since he spoke Kissi and two other local languages of the two neighbouring states.

While he did this, *The Tablet* began a serialisation of the documents in ten solid Saturday slots which further heightened the problems of the regime and its loyal associates. The series was called the 'Russian Saga'. The Russian Saga created journalistic history in Sierra Leone. For the first time in the political history of the country, the editor of a newspaper was summoned to appear before a committee of parliamentarians in order to answer key questions. That editor, of course, was Peter Fornell. The episode marked the beginning of the muzzling of the free press (such as it was), and with it any person sympathising with its 'propaganda' and 'lies'.

9

Diamonds Without Frontiers

Diamonds from Sierra Leone are unique. They know no frontiers. Since time immemorial they have been smuggled across the Sierra Leone/Liberia frontier into Monrovia, Guinea, Europe and the Middle East. In the year 2000, the United Nations, USA and the European Union dubbed them 'blood diamonds' and banned their smuggling, at least on paper, so as to put an end to Sierra Leone's civil war.

Fallah Buedu, sent to Monrovia in order to investigate the *modus operandi* of the smuggling cartel, threw light on two salient points: a lack of patriotism among Sierra Leoneans, and the causal relationship between blood diamonds and a future war. He had no idea that this war was coming, but it did, and it lasted twelve years, killed thousands, maimed thousands, created a battalion of child soldiers as young as five, and disrupted the structures of state and society. In brief, blood diamonds are Sierra Leone's nemesis.

However, from an Africa-wide point of view it is not exclusively a typical Sierra Leonean problem. To a large extent, it constitutes the chronic culture of self-destruction that characterises the dark national character of most of Africa's failed states. In Nigeria, oil constitutes that country's nemesis, and war-torn Angola and the Democratic Republic of the Congo have similar problems, to name but a few states where national problems have been fuelled by the brutal effects of dictatorship and the greed inherent in the redistribution of the wealth derived from natural resources.

The Dukor Hotel in downtown Monrovia was the business home of smugglers and dealers in blood diamonds and gold. Prior to the civil war in Liberia, this magnificent hotel stood elegantly on the top of an elevated hill and over-looked this ancient city in West Africa. Its citizens detest the idea that it was a colony, though historical accounts testify rightly that it was formerly colonised by the Americans. Its rich and affluent political leaders from the late presidents Tubman and Tolbert onwards were Americo-Liberian freed slaves. They built a political dynasty following the country's independence in 1847 and asserted a firm grip on political power. But in 1980 an insignificant native, Master Sergeant Samuel Kayon Doe, turned petty dictator, and the dynasty and the power that went with it crumbled.

The executive areas of this cosmopolitan city used to boast of giant edifices such as the Temple of Justice, the Firestone Building and the Dukor International Hotel prior to the mass killings and destruction in the 1980s. The architectural influence on these buildings reflected the American colonial connection with Liberia. Liberia even plagiarised the Declaration of Independence!

From the exclusively cosy rooms of the Dukor International Hotel, international smugglers of all sorts of nationalities spread their commercial influence and power in Africa, Europe and the Middle East. While the foreign dealers and smugglers utilised the money to build their nations, most Sierra Leoneans deposited the proceeds into Swiss bank accounts.

For example, sources close to President Siato, a major chief patron of illicit smuggling throughout his reign, often talked about how he deposited millions of dollars of blood diamonds into a Swiss bank. And because the details were codified and kept top secret between him and his bankers, when he died Sierra Leone lost the savings to the owners of the bank. Had the diamonds not been smuggled in the first place and the savings retrieved by the state of Sierra Leone after Siato's death, the money would have saved millions of starving Sierra Leoneans, built well-equipped educational institutions, created jobs and above all averted the bloody civil war. It was a manifestation of naked greed and unpatriotic madness!

Before he left Sierra Leone, Fallah Buedu had received vital tips from Alphonsus Kamara, Mahmud Hassan Mahmud, a Lebanese businessman, and Sajor Bah, a Guinean national business tycoon. The latter was a specialist smuggler in international cigarettes and electronic tape-recorders. He shuttled between Koindu, Buedu, Kono, Liberia, Guinea and Europe, evading millions of dollars worth of customs duties and taxes with impunity through the support of the smuggling godfathers.

Alphonsus was much more comfortable with Fallah Buedu than with the Chief Editor of the paper, simply because he was a blood relative of a senior member of the very regime that they sought to bring down, which Alphonsus considered an act of double standards and unpalatable. So he confided more in Fallah Buedu.

Once Fallah Buedu found himself on the shores of Liberia, he kept his identity secret from all and sundry except his contact people. So, Fallah dressed in Muslim clothing: a white gown, kaftan and sacred veil, similar to those worn only by the holiest of holies according to the tenets of Islam. Light in complexion and heavily bearded, Fallah could easily pass for any Middle Eastern national, so his disguise was secure.

In order to lessen the burden of his task, Alphonsus had contacted his main source at the office of the Sierra Leone High Commission in Monrovia. She was Marion Aligalie, a girlfriend of his at Furah Bay College. Marion was the eldest daughter of the Imam of one of the most important mosques in Freetown, the Fullah Town Central Mosque.

Marion had also had a brief romantic spell with Mahmud Hassan Mahmud. It proved financially rewarding for her and her parents. The Middle Eastern smuggler purchased acres of land and houses for her parents around Winkinson Road, one of the posh areas in Freetown. But she ditched him for the High Commissioner, her boss, who promised to marry her. Her decision was also informed by the fact that Mahmud's funds dried up dramatically beyond belief at a time when she was in dire need of financial assistance.

Unfortunately, Dr Thaimu Sankoh, the High Commissioner, disappointed her and married someone from his own tribe, a Limba of middle-class parentage. This disappointment put Marion through dreadful pains and for some years she suffered from post-traumatic stress. She could hardly come to terms with the fact that the High Commissioner of all people had ditched her after an engagement ceremony held at the Dukor Hotel. It was attended by the *crème de la crème* of that land and generated huge publicity and media interest, which vibrated across the borders of the sister states of Sierra Leone, Liberia and Guinea.

70

However, despite his public rejection of her, they remained lovers. Ironically, he didn't realise that Marion had an ulterior motive for keeping up their fragile relationship at a casual level. Of course, she kept it limping along so as to punish His Excellency for bringing shame on her and her family. She wasn't in a hurry; she would wait as long as it took. Fortunately, she had many of the High Commissioner's secrets and those of his high profile associates in her palm.

The Commissioner was the key middleman and facilitator of the triangular deals transacted between a group of Sierra Leonean Lebanese, ministers, top civil servants, Israelis and Europeans. They smuggled diamonds from Sierra Leone and took them to Europe and the Middle East via Liberia.

Fallah and *The Tablet* came up with a neat plan to unravel the facts, according to which he was to pose as a rich illicit Middle Eastern diamond smuggler and broker based in Koidu. His main storyline would be that he and his business partner Mahmud Hassan Mahmud had been double-crossed by the High Commissioner and two Israelis. For obvious reasons, Marion Aligalie would not take this unkindly; she would fall for such a ploy easily and it would harden her resolve for the revenge she had craved for so many years.

And this was the reason why. Her relationship with Hassan fell to pieces because he failed to pay the university tuition fees of three of her brothers, undergraduate students at Oxford University in England. What happened was that Mahmud Hassan Mahmud was made bankrupt because a super smuggling deal in which he invested all his savings plus bank loans and overdrafts was squandered by the High Commissioner and three Israelis, after which he went broke. But Marion didn't buy his story at that time, and besides, she had other distractions, so they parted company.

Hassan was not only angry; he was petrified because the High Commissioner's accomplices were Israeli Jews, his Middle Eastern sworn enemies. So for five years he waited for the opportune time when he could have his revenge. Hence, there were two embittered people locked in a sworn conspiracy to wreak vengeance on the High Commissioner – Marion and Mahmud Hassan Mahmud.

Two weeks had passed since Christmas but the office of the Sierra Leone High Commission in Monrovia was still on holiday. The High Commissioner and his wife Mariatu were away in the Middle East and London, apparently to sell his own collection of gems accumulated over several years, the mining of which he had illicitly financed and solicited in Yengema, one of the richest diamond enclaves in the Kono District.

Marion stayed in Monrovia to take care of the daily routines of the office, including diamond and passport deals in His Excellency's absence. She worked comfortably from her official residence, near Tubman International Airport in Downtown Monrovia.

Passports were crucial to the deals in illicit diamonds. Without the use of passports the deals scored little or no success. This was how passports were utilised to expedite the deals: foreign nationals engaged in the deals were given Sierra Leonean ordinary, service and diplomatic passports to enhance their trips safely and easily across immigration, police and customs checks. As for the deals involving the President and his team of ministers, the High Commissioner codified these 'Pr/MD', meaning Presidium, Ministerial Deals. He used the diplomatic bag to claim diplomatic immunity at checkpoints and airports. The same strategy was applied to accomplish his personal deals. They were code named 'HP', meaning High Priority.

This diplomat was an incredibly greedy and gullible creature, and he hardly trusted anyone. For him, cheating was a religion, an art the success of which depended on self-discipline at the highest level. He was a master cheat, second only to the chief patron of all cheats in the land, President Siato. Above all, he was instinctively inspired by the proverbial saying of his one-time religious education and Latin teacher at the St Francis Secondary School, Makeni: 'a man's best servant is himself'. Meticulously, he put all the precautions in place and closed all the loopholes. 'You have to close all the windows as well as the doors and avoid any alibi', he would often say to Marion, his sweet-heart, when their game was at its climax. The spoils were huge: multi-million dollar mansions acquired in London, America, Bo, Makeni and Freetown; fleets of expensive cars; the most beautiful women; and huge bank accounts in Switzerland and London.

The implications of his acts were irreparable. They were economically devastating and brought national disgrace to bear on the country. First, you had rich, organised and highly influential foreign nationals masquerading with Sierra Leonean travel documents as ordinary Sierra Leoneans and diplomats whose key objective was to impoverish the country with impunity. While they enriched their own countries, Sierra Leone was ripped off, its God-given wealth drained away. Second, it was disgraceful and disappointing that Sierra Leoneans educated by taxpayers' money and put in high positions of trust connived with foreign nationals to defraud and impoverish their own country.

History also had it that prior to the Lebanese civil war, one of the Lebanese smugglers who made fortunes out of Sierra Leone diamonds actually built one of the most beautiful mansions in the Lebanese capital *Beirut*, which was later used as one of the offices of the warring factions. He was so excited that he named it after the Capital of Sierra Leone: 'Freetown'. But as the Lord would have it the building collapsed under the heavy bombardment of mortars and machine-guns used by rival militias. Another story had it that the proceeds from Sierra Leonean blood diamonds financed the Lebanese civil war. According to the story, ten of the smugglers spent blood diamonds to finance the Christian militias.

When he arrived in Monrovia, Fallah went straight to the premises of Marion. That evening, the diplomat was busy tidying up, putting together the paperwork, the deals, making the necessary phone calls, and chasing payments on behalf of her unscrupulous boss and members of the smuggling cartel. Her little niece, Yatunde, was in her room, next to the main door.

Fallah knocked repeatedly on the door as instructed by Alphonsus and Mahmud Hassan Mahmud.

'There is someone at the door!' shouted Yatunde. She was frightened; more so because she had never seen someone in Middle Eastern attire come to the premises. The only regular visitors she had ever set eyes on since she joined her aunt from Freetown were the High Commissioner and Mahmud Hassan Mahmud.

Marion came to the door, opened it immediately and greeted Fallah with an overwhelming familiarity which was rather surprising for her little niece, who thought that her aunt should have exercised some caution before letting the man in, being a stranger. Poor, innocent girl! She didn't know the power of the smuggling cartel and the love webs in which her aunt was entangled. She was notorious and greedily spread her passion across the whole region – the Republics of Liberia, Guinea and Sierra Leone. How she managed the competition that revolved around her and the inherent conflicts of interest, only her Maker could know!

'How was your trip, from Kono? The roads are bad these days eh?' she asked Fallah with a broad smile of familiarity.

'Well, peace be unto Muhammad, the gracious, benevolent and merciful. Also peace be unto Allah, the creator. Thanks and praise be unto both for they saw me through the rough mountains, high seas, hurricanes and rough roads. And now, miraculously, here I am sitting in this beautiful mansion in the presence of the most beautiful creature Allah has ever let me set eyes on. May Allah be praised, Amen!'

Marion was moved by the rich religious oratory of the Kissi journalist, dressed in the robes of a Middle Eastern cleric. The words sounded like a romantic poem in her ears. The last time she had heard such beautiful, soul-touching and inspiring lines was when she and Alphonsus studied classics and poetry at the university.

Ironically, Fallah was not aware that Marion had been given his entire profile and that she was part and parcel of an insider plot to expose His Excellency, the High Commissioner.

They had dinner together, after which she advised Fallah to get some rest before their important discussions began.

'You will retire now and have some rest. I will do the same. Then at one o'clock in the morning I shall wake you up and we'll spend some hours together.' She gave him a nod and added, 'I hope you will be ready, as we have a lot to talk about!'

Obviously, he was excited. Success here would be the biggest breakthrough of his career. He was so overwhelmed by the anticipated success of his mission that he hardly slept. He lay on the bed and talked to himself continuously as he waited for the clock to strike exactly one o'clock.

His hostess on the other hand had only a short and troubled sleep. She dreamt about the High Commissioner and his wife in a romantic mood. She woke up, absolutely disgusted. 'Why, for Christ's sake, why? He is all yours now, why bother me any more, do you want to finish me off?' She reached immediately for one of the dozens of bottles of concoctions hidden under her bed and sprinkled the contents all over her body. Her parents sent this particular one for her. She acquired the others with huge fortunes in Guinea and Monrovia. They were meant for her personal protection against harm and evil, to inspire luck and good fortune.

She was worried by the dream because in African traditional beliefs if a woman dreams of her lover's wife, that lady is conjuring the evils of darkness against her.

Like all journalists, Fallah thought that he should not leave anything to chance, so he took the necessary precautions. He hid a small pocket tape-recorder in one of the pockets of his big gown. It had been given to him by Alpha Jalloh two years ago; an upright businessman, and resident of Buedu, Kissi Tongi, the very hometown of the journalist.

At one o'clock in the morning, when the entire Monrovia city went to sleep, the two set to work. Marion took Fallah Buedu down to the pantry, which was attached to the main building next to the garage. She fed the curious journalist with vital documentary and oral evidence. It confirmed some of the information that Alphonsus had given to *The Tablet* in Freetown. He recorded every word of the conversation, which lasted for three hours. It was nerve-racking,

76

and Marion had consumed almost a bottle of whisky by the end. She divulged all the secrets of the High Commissioner who had ruined her life.

At one stage she sobbed heavily. Apparently, she was suffering from mixed emotions of joy and frustration. On the one hand she was happy because she had had the opportunity for revenge at last. On the other, she was very much aware of the wider ramifications: she may have cost herself her job.

At the end of the session, they both went to sleep. Marion woke up late, but the journalist was up very early in the morning, a routine he'd religiously practised for almost two decades. After lunch he went to meet his second contact at the Dukor International Hotel. He was a middle-aged retired Brigadier. He had been in self-exile since the SLPP had fallen from grace in 1967. He was Brigadier Donald Lansin, an easterner. He had a political extradition order to Sierra Leone in order to be court-martialled hanging over his head. The Brigadier was not the only political victim forced to take shelter in Liberia; with him were two former ministers of the collapsed government. They hailed from the Jawai Chiefdom, Daru, in the Kailahun District. There is no place like home, home, sweet home, so they kept in constant touch with political developments in Sierra Leone. They were almost mourning when the journalist arrived at the hotel that afternoon. They had bad news from Freetown. Someone had smuggled two recent newspaper publications from Sierra Leone in the same diplomatic bag that ferried blood diamonds across the frontiers. They were *The Tablet* and the *We Yone* newspapers. The latter was a pro-government paper. Its frustrating headline was particularly intriguing and had a considerable impact on the men:

77

BRAVO, BRAVO, THE MOLE OF THE RUSSIAN SAGA DISCOVERED!

The Tablet carried a rather mild headline:

WHO IS THE RUSSIAN MOLE?
PLEASE ASK MOSCOW!

How dramatically things can change in an uncertain world, only God knows! In seconds, Fallah's mood of happiness changed dramatically and left him with the most unpleasant feelings in his life, since he had started putting pen to paper. He read the papers briefly, almost shaking. He had little or no discussion of importance with the Brigadier, who was in tears as they reflected on the after-effects, should the source of the Russian Saga truly be brought to light. Fallah tried more than ten times that day to phone Alphonsus in Freetown, but unfortunately he didn't get through. It was the same old story again: the chronic disease of underdevelopment manifested by bad road networks, infrastructures and rusty telephone lines had locked the two neighbouring countries in utter darkness and communication blackouts.

The mission came to an end after three weeks. There was no doubt that after the undercover investigation Fallah was equipped with the necessary weapons, which he and *The Tablet* could have used as the last nail in the coffin of the most unpopular regime in modern African history. But after reading the *We Yone* paper, he was left with mixed feelings. To his mind, the contents of the publication apparently indicated that developments may have obtained in his absence which would let neither the sensitive issue of the Russian Saga, nor the outcome of the undercover investigations in the Republic of Liberia, see daylight.

10

Operation Lethal Weapon

When Fallah Buedu learned towards the end of his mission in Monrovia that the mole of the Russian Saga had been named in his absence, he prayed fervently that night for a favourable outcome to his undercover investigation. Unfortunately, it was not to be. Under duress, Mahmud Hassan Mahmud, one of his key informants, had not only leaked the identity of the Russian Saga informer, but also informed the authorities about Fallah's mission to Monrovia. The regime was waiting for his return. The government set up a committee to deal with the matter in a drastic manner that truly characterised its ruthless credentials.

'It is high time we put an end to this virus of misinformation and journalistic distortions being spread around the four corners of this country by *The Tablet*,' said the Rt Honourable Winston Conteh, Speaker of the House of Parliament. The Speaker and the Force Commander of the armed forces of Sierra Leone discussed their strategy to gag *The Tablet*. They held their meeting in the notorious Committee Room number 1967 of the Parliament building in Freetown.

History repeated itself and the autocratic credentials of the regime were set to complete a full cycle. For it was in Committee Room 1967 that the Speaker, then a senior member of the Central Committee of the APC, and the Force Commander, who was at the time third in command of the army, had held an important meeting to work out the policies that would keep the APC in power indefinitely. The First Vice President, the overall party strategist, chaired that meeting. It was in 1967, against the backdrop of the controversial general election result that brought them to power. After that historic meeting they named the room '1967' in order to commemorate their political victory over the SLPP.

It was in Committee Room 1967 that a devilish plan was designed and executed. It led to the massacre of hundreds of helpless citizens in a blazing inferno at the Gingerhall, in the east end of Freetown. There was no valid reason for the carnage except that the victims exercised their democratic rights by voting against an autocratic regime.

This same room had hosted several crucial talks that stopped numerous Students Union demonstrations and mini-strikes by the Sierra Leone Labour Congress and Sierra Leone Teachers Union in the 1970s and 80s. Most of the meetings were initiated and chaired by the First Vice President, the mastermind and supreme party strategist.

This time, it was the turn of the Speaker and the Force Commander to initiate and execute a comprehensive plan that would gag the only free newspaper in the country. It was a Herculean task, but they were both quite equal to it.

They drew up a four-fold strategy and code named it 'Operation Lethal Weapon'. First, they would summon the editor of the paper, the brave Peter Fornell, before a parliamentary committee and warn him to stop the publication of the Russian Saga forthwith. Then they would put him under pressure to confirm the evidence of Mahmud Hassan Mahmud. Finally, if the committee failed to interrogate the editor properly and extract the vital information relating to the Russian Saga and the undercover investigation by Fallah Buedu, they would unleash a reign of terror on a scale that the nation had not witnessed since Gingerhall.

The regime had a comprehensive and formidable machinery of thuggery and vandalism put in place, so implementing the final aspect of the plan wasn't a problem. For instance, they had members of the APC Youth Brigade, and the Internal Security Unit (ISU), who were ready to do anything just to maintain the status quo.

The ISU was notorious for creating mayhem. It was a formidable party paramilitary force. Its members were trained in Cuba and neighbouring Guinea. The ISU was put in place the moment the APC gained power, primarily to put down rebellions against the regime. Critics often dismissed the ISU as a disruptive private army of retainers that were overpaid to kill off genuine democratic opposition in Sierra Leone.

But the overall status of the ISU in the eyes of the party supremo went beyond such simplistic connotations. Its creation was inspired by the lack of trust between the regime and the army. When the regime came to power they discovered a link between their predecessor, the SLPP, and the top brass of the army, so they were obsessed with its demise. There were even strong rumours in the inner circles of the regime that there was a plan to replace the army with the ISU. Since then, the government had sought to undermine the credibility of the army and nurture a possible replacement – the ISU.

By the late 1970s, the status of the army was similar to a toothless political bulldog that could only bark, but hardly had the pedigree to bite anything. It was a spent force; the

ISU was now virtually the powerhouse of national security. It was a risky political strategy, but a ruthless regime like the APC considered it plausible.

The senior cadres of the ISU were party loyalists, trusted relatives and friends of ministers and the Presidium. Its power and elevated status was manifested when Sierra Leone hosted the Organization of African Unity (OAU) summit. While the personnel of a weakened, beleaguered army were made to parade the streets of Freetown with empty guns without a single bullet, even for the sake of self-defence, the notorious ISU were seen in every corner, not only in the most expensive and smart kit, but carrying Soviet automatic AK47 rifles, fully loaded with brand-new bullets.

Above all, the ISU were authorised by presidential decree to kill without warning throughout the period of the most expensive political summit ever held in Sierra Leone.

Due to its brutal credentials and thirst for blood, the ISU were known as 'lethal weapons'. Critics muttered that ISU stood for 'I shoot you'.

The details of the meeting were compiled immediately into a comprehensive dossier and the Speaker took this by hand to the State House for the perusal of the President. The latter gave his approval of the strategy, but added a further and lethal clause. He ordered that anyone found within the offices of *The Tablet*, including the two editors, must be shot dead.

The news leaked in the public domain as soon as it was concluded and spread throughout the land. But the full contents of the deadly strategy were kept secret by the regime. They would take the paper and the nation by surprise!

Similar to the uneven contest between David and Goliath narrated in the biblical stories, news of the pending encounter between the regime and the two editors generated a lot of interest. The validity and merits of the bizarre decision of the regime were debated in wine bars, bus huts and offices. Above all, the populace were very concerned that the government's motive was to put a lid on the mouth of the last bastion of democracy in the country.

As they drank and talked in pubs and their homes, the depressed citizens spoke for the first time in public since they had inherited a corrupt and autocratic regime about a national rebellion, a revolt to bring the government down if it attempted to kill off the paper, their only voice and watchdog. At the Sunny Mark, two gentlemen talked about the divine status of the *The Tablet* and how determined they were to bring down the regime, if it gagged the paper.

'This is crazy, it's like bringing back Hitler from the dead so as to spill more blood. For most of us, *The Tablet* is more than an ordinary newspaper. It is our *vox populi*. It is the voice and conscience of a downtrodden populace. Gagging it means muzzling us.'

'We shall fight tooth and nail in order to stop this madness,' replied his colleague, who wore a smart black suit and a white shirt, marking him out as a wealthy business-man. In reality, he worked as a banking executive at the Sierra Leone Commercial Bank, at the bottom of Walpole Street, close to the US embassy.

It was his birthday and it coincided with the good news that he was to go on transfer to Koidu town and head the branch of the Commercial Bank there. Koidu town was the home of the precious diamonds that enriched Lebanese businesses, foreign brokers and government cartels. The banker drank happily at the good news of his transfer to the melting pot of Koidu. For he would have the oppor-tunity to enrich himself via bribes from customers and other illicit endeavours. As a branch manager in this lucrative region, he would have a whole vault full of money at his disposal, out of which he could finance illicit mining as well as international smuggling. At the end of each transaction, he would replenish the vault and retain the huge profits. It was illegal, but it was the rule of the game throughout the nation. Each time he thought of these prospects to amass wealth at his new station, he leaped for joy, ordered more drinks and gave more tips to the bar attendant.

At the other end of the pub sat a poor student from Furah Bay College, University of Sierra Leone. He drank slowly and spent almost three hours sipping a pint of beer offered by a freelance reporter. He was poor, jobless and penniless. He was dressed in worn out jeans, the threads of which were so transparent that one could see his skin and buttocks. And most disappointing was his fate at the university. His studies were not going well, and his future was bleak.

The student was Denis Turay. The nation had thousands of youths that suffered a similar fate to Denis. This particular one had failed his qualifying year undergraduate examinations, had taken a resit and was awaiting the results. Exam results at that time were often released late. Sometimes they were published as late as November or December, two months after the beginning of the new academic year. To make matters worse, students awaiting resit results did not receive any student allowance.

Denis was not a good student, and so he fell in that unfortunate category. Worst of all, his case was a peculiar one because he came from a poor background, so the prospect of offering sweeteners and backhanders to unscrupulous lecturers or college administrative staff in order to gain extra marks or pass grades was extremely remote.

Thus, in the absence of hard work throughout his studies there was little he could do to survive at college. As he sat on the rusty bench and killed off time, these facts tormented him. He listened carefully to the conversation between the two men and decided to contribute, using his knowledge of political science, his subject.

He said, 'Freedom, democracy and human rights are precious commodities. They are priceless and worth fighting for at all costs. But they are not earned cheaply. It is fine to talk about taking up arms against this regime, but who will spearhead the revolution?'

'What, take up arms? Who said anything about taking up arms? In fact, did we ever mention the word "arms" I think not! Please, don't misquote us!' reproached the bank manager.

'Well, that is precisely the point. How are you going to boot out a regime just by debating the issues over pints of beer? Mind you, revolution needs serious planning; it takes time, self-sacrifice. But here you are, scared to death just at the mention of the key words "revolution" and "arms". That begs the salient question: would you ever have the guts, the tenacity, to get rid of this deadly, bloodthirsty regime?' Denis pushed his chair towards the two men. But when he got closer they lost interest in the conversation.

'Please, please, don't implicate us!' said the bank manager's friend. 'We never said we were going to bring down any regime. We are just here to have good time, OK?' Then he collected his change from the bar attendant and left.

This was the trend throughout the era of political and socioeconomic despair in Sierra Leone. For three decades, the President and his henchmen basked in opulence and wealth while the populace suffered. The reason was simple – in the absence of an organised civil society, autocratic regimes will remain in power indefinitely unless someone is ready to take responsibility. Unfortunately, in Siato's Sierra Leone, the sad reality was that there was no one ready to take up that responsibility. In fact, they dismissed the idea as a big risk that was not worth taking, considering the nature and autocratic credentials of the regime.

Operation Lethal Weapon swung into action on a Saturday. First, Fornell was summoned to the Criminal Investigation Department (CID) headquarters in Freetown. He was asked a number of questions, after which he was finally released and ordered according to presidential decree to appear before the parliamentary committee on Monday at 10 a.m.

When he returned to the office he summoned an emergency meeting of the inner circle of *The Tablet* staff. It was held on the balcony of Sunny Mark due to the fact that their office was not suitable for such a sensitive meeting. There was no privacy at all; it was very busy and often overcrowded, due to the comings and goings throughout the day. And in Siato's Sierra Leone, the culture of a police state set a cross-section of the population against one another. The regime virtually put a knife through the values that held civil society together. There were huge rewards in exchange for information, which everyone fought very hard to grab at the slightest opportunity. The regime dished out money like water to informants from all walks of life.

The emergency meeting kicked off with pints of beers and tots of whisky as a means of inspiration. An elderly man in his sixties from Moyamba poured a libation to the gods and ancestral spirits. He prayed for prosperity, victory over their adversaries and protection. Then the Deputy Editor of the paper, Hinga Taylor, opened the proceedings. He had been President of the Students' Union when they were at college. He used his position to reach out to the poor and radical students in the western area of Freetown and criticised the regime at National Union of Students summits.

But his efforts did not change the regime and nor did they make civil society any braver or help to organise and inspire mass demonstrations, sufficient to shake the fabric of government. He was not comfortable with the presidential decree. *The Tablet* was being placed on trial, a trial that would put an end to any press freedom in Sierra Leone. He believed they must defy the decree.

'I believe, from the bottom of my heart, comrade,' he said to Fornell, 'that you should not attend this meeting in parliament. And this is why: according to Section 27, Subsection 4 of the 1961 constitution, such presidential decrees are invalid, unless there is a state of emergency, and at present there is not. Thus, it is flawed and a travesty of justice.'

The marked difference between the two men was that Fornell was a believer in the ideology of 'non-violent action'. His obsession with the texts and ideals of freedom fighters like Steve Biko, Gandhi, Martin Luther King Jr and a host of moderates had shaped his thoughts. His colleague, on the other hand, was the Walter Rodney type – he believed in taking issues by the scruff of the neck. They should fight the presidential decree. Attending the meeting would be interpreted by the populace as compromising their position. It was the last thing they should contemplate, considering the level of trust and hope the people had in them.

He spoke calmly, hoping to persuade Fornell. 'Comrade,

you know as well as I that this is not a legitimate regime, nor is the parliamentary group they have ordered us to appear before legal. It is a cabal. And any free, law-abiding citizen should not obey orders from any cabal, nor should they give in even at gunpoint. We are benevolent liberals, so resistance must be our weapon against this unscrupulous regime.'

'Nevertheless, I think we should attend this meeting, comrade. Whatever happens, history will not judge this regime kindly,' replied Fornell.

In the end they decided that they would both attend the meeting.

When they arrived on that fateful Monday they met hundreds of students and a handful of trade unionists outside. They all carried colourful banners, in support of the journalists. It was an encouraging welcome that demonstrated bravery and a faith in the paper. Sadly, they didn't know that violence would take precedence over sanity and that their banners, symbols of democracy, wouldn't make any difference in the face of the mayhem, the turmoil that lay in wait for them.

Twenty minutes later, at exactly 10.45 a.m., six trucks loaded with armed personnel, mostly the notorious ISU, arrived. The men wore riot uniforms and were equipped with assault rifles, smoke guns and live bullets. They took up position immediately and waited for the order from the commanding officer.

As the two journalists made their way into the building, they were greeted by sounds of thunderous applause from the crowd. They waved their colourful banners full of liberal phrases and slogans. 'Liberty, Free Press or Death' read one of them. 'Sons of Hope, Inspiration and Liberty, We Will Die for You!' read another.

Then, suddenly, the colourful scene of hope and euphoria was overtaken by a terrible, gloomy cloud of despair. The battle lines were drawn. Twelve huge men dressed in army fatigue uniforms ran towards the journalists to drag them away, but the mob managed to rescue them from their kidnappers. Whether this action was in the interests of the journalists was uncertain!

The ISU opened fire immediately at what the commander later described as a 'hostile crowd'. They killed two and wounded many more. The dead were both in their early twenties. Some of the protesters couldn't stand the carnage, so they ran for it. The paramilitary troops pursued them relentlessly. As they ran down the hill they shot into the crowd as well as into the air. The chaos spread and for a while the busy overcrowded streets of Freetown came to a halt. There were even rumours that the city had woken up to another military coup.

While the poor, innocent protesters lay dead in a pool of their own blood, the editors were later dragged into the notorious Committee Room 1967 and faced the second phase of their ordeal.

The committee of MPs interrogated the editors rigorously for hours and warned them to stop the serialisation of the Russian Saga immediately. They also applied pressure on the men to confirm the source of the Saga. But the determined, brave editors refused to corroborate the evidence of Mahmud Hassan Mahmud. They could not betray Alphonsus Kamara, their source. At their meeting in Bo Kakowa, Alphonsus, the mole of the Russian Saga, had implored them under oath to keep his name secret.

At the end of the tight interrogation the committee forced both editors to sign documents that would implicate them in the future. They had no choice, so they complied.

In the face of all the drama and violence, the stubborn crowds refused to go away and abandon their heroes to the wolves. They waited for them at the foot of the hill. Meanwhile, the bodies of the innocent men were rushed to the Connaught Hospital, in order to conceal the evidence from a BBC reporter, Oneil Thompson, the only international pressman in the country.

Eventually, the two editors were released and the jubilant crowds surged forward and carried them shoulder-high to the centre of Freetown. In less than five minutes they were joined by thousands at the Sunny Mark, the only shrine of free expression in the city. The jubilant crowds barricaded the streets and kicked off a street party in celebration. As they drank, they chanted 'Damn the thuggery and corruption, let democracy reign!'

Generously they drank, and proposed endless toasts to the health, determination and bravery of the two journalists. The toasts were punctuated by speeches glorifying their heroism and goodwill for their country and poor compatriots.

Unfortunately, the celebrations didn't last long. Another cocktail of mayhem was unleashed by the regime after five days. It was on a Saturday morning and the skies of Freetown were overcast, which reflected the shadows of the coming events. And when they came the impact was devastating; they affected the psyche of the entire nation. On that fateful morning, the offices of *The Tablet* were vandalised.

But first, Fallah Buedu was placed under arrest by a group of secret service policemen as early as two o'clock in the morning, the moment he crossed the final checkpoint at Toradu. Mahmud Hassan Mahmud had given them the relevant information.

Then came the deadly hour. At exactly 5.30 in the morning, a group of thugs backed by masked armed men raided the offices of *The Tablet* and smashed all their printing machines and typewriters. They killed two of the regular paperboys who had come to collect the Saturday edition. The two boys had distributed the paper for five years, every Saturday, but on that day they met their death.

The cold-blooded killings had a massive impact on the course of democracy in the country. They further dented the reputation of the regime. Above all the death of the two innocent boys represented a gloomy sunset in the troubled history of Sierra Leone.

As for the two editors, they survived. As if the gods were on their side, they were not in the buildings during the attack. Prior to it, they had done all the printing late at night, and organised all the papers for the newsagents as well as their regular paperboys, to collect and sell in the morning.

Luckily, after the work, they went to a birthday party at Furah Bay. The party went on till 4.30 in the morning, so they decided to pass the remaining hours of the night in the premises of their host.

The raid took place as they slept. As a matter of fact, Fornell actually dreamt about the incident and had several nightmares. At one point he woke up, horrified, shouting, 'Stop, don't shoot! Blood, blood on your hands!'

Other people were woken by his screams, but they took no notice. He was drunk, or else hung over, or a bit of both. So they went back to bed.

Operation Lethal Weapon was over, it had served its dreadful purpose: brutalised the *Tablet*, and muzzled the last bastion of democracy throughout the land. The editors were lucky to escape with their lives. They fled immediately to the United States of America. Then after six months they claimed political asylum and became American citizens.

As for Alphonsus Kamara, their comrade in arms fled the country after the dust of anarchy had settled. Through the help of Marion Aligalie, he was smuggled into Monrovia and later flew to London. He too claimed political asylum on arrival at Heathrow Airport. Political asylum granted, Alphonsus Kamara enjoyed the protection of Her Majesty's government.

At least in their respective adopted countries, the three men enjoyed liberty and justice, priceless liberal values their native land, Sierra Leone failed to offer her citizens in the gloomy days of the APC regime.

Sadly, the regime carried on, while the minds of the people slept against the awful reality of their situation. It was indeed a dark sunset for Sierra Leone.